Bangkok Bound

By

Shane Wiggand

Dedication

To my bestfriend.

About the author

Shane Wiggand is a former pro Thai boxer and a MMA fighter. He lived, trained, and worked in Thailand for 10 years. Shane now owns on a small farm in Tennessee with his goats, dogs, and chickens.

Table of Contents

__Introduction__

Isabella walked into Xander's life 7 years ago when she became one of his students at his kickboxing gym. Within a couple of weeks, Xander and Isabella's friendship blossomed as the two started hanging out almost every day, which turned into a romance. Two years into their relationship, Xander's business partner caused him to almost go bankrupt, losing his home and most of his finances. Isabella graciously stepped in and offered Xander to move in with her parents until he could get back on his feet financially. A few months later, Xander was able to purchase some land out in the countryside. Their future goal was for the two of them to have an off-grid homestead and a place to keep all their animals. Over time, living with Isabella's parents and going out to their farm every day to feed the animals started to put unnecessary pressure on their relationships. Unable to rent a home because of all the animals. Xander and Isabella decided to move into their unfinished cabin over the summer. Xander promised that he would have the cabin done in no time. However, due to the weather, being exhausted from his job, and financially set back from his construction business, the cabin was way off schedule. Xander could see that Isabella was getting upset more often due to poor living conditions. Xander lived in Thailand for many years and always wanted to take Isabella there.

So, in July, Xander buys tickets to Bangkok for Isabella's birthday the following spring. Two months later, Isabella's frustrations reach a boiling point. Calling it quits and moving back in with her parents. After a few months of giving Isabella a little space, he was able to convince Isabella to continue with the trip in March if they only went as friends.

Chapter 1: Lost Bag

"This is your Captain Speaking. We will touch down in 20 minutes at Bangkok's Suvarnabhumi Airport at 10:52 pm. We hope you had a wonderful flight with us. At this time, please put your seats and trays up in their upright position. Flight Attendants, please make your final rounds".

Xander takes off his headphones and gently wakes Izzy up. "Isabelle. Isabelle. Isabelle. It's time to wake up." She slowly wakes up from using his shoulder as a pillow. "You need to put your seat up. We are landing in 20 minutes."

Isabelle still seems half asleep. "Can I have the rest of your water and what time is it?" she yawns.

"It's about 10:30 pm Thailand time." He responds.

As she finishes the water, she asks, "What do we do when we land?"

Xander answers, "Just follow me," as a big smile appears.

"What was that crazy smile about? Do you think I can go pee before we land?" She asks.

"I think you can if there is not a big line. Maybe ask the flight attendant," before he finishes his sentence, she quickly jumps up and looks at the bathrooms mid-cabin and rear. She quickly walks to the rear of the plane as she notices the bathroom door opens.

A few minutes later, Isabelle returns to her seat. She looks at Xander and yells, "What the Hell! Why didn't you tell me my mascara was smeared all over and my hair, looking crazy?"

"Well, you've only been up for a few moments, and then you jumped up and ran to the bathroom," Xander responds. She sits down, puts her seat belt on, and grabs the magazine from the seat folder.

Xander starts to think to himself. "Maybe this wasn't a good idea for both of us to go on this trip after all. She has been upset this whole flight. I wanted this to be a happy, wonderful trip for two old friends trying at least to save a close friendship." Nothing else was said until the plane docked at the terminal.

"Please carefully open the overhead bins, as your bags could have moved during the flight." As the Caption pauses on the plane audio. "Your baggage pick up will be on carousel 43. Thank you for flying Etihad Airlines. Welcome to Bangkok."

Xander turns to Isabelle and says. "Since you are sitting on the aisle seat. You need to get up pretty fast when the seatbelt light turns off."

"Why?" She asks.

He replies, "Because everyone has been on this plane for 8 hours, and they are eager to get off. A lot of the Arab men do not respect women, and we will be one of the last people off this plane. Plus, now I need to go piss."

Isabelle blankly looks at Xander, nods, and thinks to herself.

The plane finally comes to a stop. "BING!" The seat belt light turns off.

Like a track star, Isabelle springs into action and jumps to her feet into the aisle, leaving room for Xander to slide in front of her. One of the passengers in the seat in front of Isabelle already opened the overhead compartment with Xander and Isabelle's carry-on bag. Xander grabs Isabelle's bag, hands it to her, and then grabs his.

Xander looks at Isabelle and says. "We finally made it!"

Isabelle smiles and asks, "What's next?" "Do we pick up our check bag or get our passport stamped?"

3

Xander answers, "We have to get our passport stamped first. Just follow me. Many other planes will be landing, and the queue for the line can become very long. But I need to use the bathroom."

11:30 pm, Xander and Isabelle arrive at the queue area for immigration. An Immigration official points to them and then directs them to line 4.

Isabelle leans over and says, "Wow! "There are a lot of people in front of us. I hope it doesn't take long. I'm so exhausted and have a bad headache. This is a long 24 hours." As she takes out her Lonely Planet book about Bangkok.

Isabelle puts the book down after about 15 minutes of reading. "It's making my headache worse." She says. "Hope we don't get caught in any of those crazy traffic jams you mentioned."

"March is not the rainy season, so we should be ok. But I've not been here in years, so I'm not sure. Looks like we are next." Says Xander.

11:51 pm, Carousel 43: Etihad 112

"Look, this is our plane here, and the bags are already spinning around," he tells Isabelle.

"I'm so ready to get to the hotel. You got 2 beds, correct? She asks.

"Yes. Yes. That's what we agreed to so you would go on this trip. Also, I requested a bathtub at the hotel. Just for you, babe," he answers.

Isabelle quickly answers back, "I'm not your babe."

"Oh, Xander! Hey, I don't see our bag. According to the monitor, that's it. I hope no one took it," she says as she looks frantically around.

"Wait right here," Xander tells Isabelle. "I see an Etihad worker. Let me ask her."

Isabelle could see Xander and Etihad Lady talking. He then looks at her, shakes his head, and walks back to her.

"This really sucks," Xander states. "Our bags are in their system. So, it means it got checked in. She said it's either in New York or Abu Dhabi. She gave me a number to call tomorrow. Do you have any extra clothes with you?"

"What the hell! Most of my stuff was in that bag. Yes, I got a few things," she angrily answered back. "How about you?"

"Yes, I got a few things," He answers. "Well, I guess we are going shopping tomorrow. Let's get a taxi and get out of here."

Rembrandt Hotel Suhumvit Soi 18. 1 am.

"As promised, we have two queen beds. And there is the tub. I'm going to take a quick shower and go to bed. I'm sure you will want to take a bath and relax. We have a big day tomorrow," Xander smiles at Isabelle. She just smiles back. He could tell something was on her mind, probably second-guessing the trip since we would only be there for a few days.

Xander exits the bathroom and says, "It's all yours. If I'm asleep when you go out, I hope you have a good night."

She says goodnight, goes into the bathroom, and locks the door.

Chapter 2: Shopping

8 am. Wake up Call.

Xander is the first to wake up and looks at Isabelle in the other bed as he thinks. "I will let her sleep a little longer. I know she doesn't like getting up early. I will go downstairs and get us some coffee."

8:28 am Xander returns to the room with the coffee. Isabelle sits in bed and looks over at Xander, holding the coffee. A smile comes over her face, and she says. "Thank you."

"You're welcome," Xander responds. "We need to get motivated. We need to get a phone while we are here. So if they find our luggage, they can call us, and we need to get a few clothes. I don't have much of anything. What type of clothes do you need? Also, we are changing hotels."

"I mostly need nighttime clothes, like if we go somewhere nice in the evening. Don't ask me any more questions until I wake up." Isabelle answers.

"Ok. Xander answers back. I'm going to take a shower, go to the lobby, and check out. Also, they can put our bags in a locker for a few hours."

Xander returns to the room 30 minutes later. Isabelle was ready to go as she jumped up and down and said "I'm so excited."

"Me too," he says back. "I guess the coffee is kicking in as he laughs." Grab your stuff. Let's get this adventure started.

9:20 am Xander and Isabelle walk out of the hotel and pass by the taxi parked on the street.

Isabelle asks Xander. "We're walking?" "Where are we going anyways?"

Xander answers, "Usually, taxis parked out in front of the hotels won't use the meter. Plus, it's about a 20 minutes or so walk."

"Oh, that's not far," she says. "But you didn't tell me where we are going."

"We are going to EmQuartier Mall." He says as he grabs Isabelle's hand.

She quickly pulls her hand away as he says. "Sorry. Old habit," as they start walking down Soi 18 towards Sukhumvit Road.

Isabelle looks around everywhere and takes in everything in amazement. As the BTS Sky train roars by overhead.

"Will we be riding this while we are here?" She asks.

Xander answers. "Yes, actually, when we get done shopping. We will take it to our hotel. Do you have a bikini with you?"

She smiles and says, "Is our hotel on the beach?"

"Nope. Sorry, but it has a really nice pool," he says, pointing to the mall.

As they enter the mall, Isabelle says, "This is the nicest mall I have ever been to."

"Wait until you see the indoor garden. It has a 3 or 4 story waterfall next to the food court." Xander answers as he looks for the directory for the Samsung Phone store. "There it is, follow me, Teerok."

She laughs.

Xander smiles and says, "We could spend hours here, but we are only here for a few days. So much more to see in this city than malls. Let's go get this phone so we can call about our bags and I'm sure you're eager to call your mom."

After walking around for about 15 minutes, they finally arrived at the Samsung store located on the 5th floor. Isabelle walks over to the windows and looks out over the city. At the same time, Xander is looking at different phones. Minutes later, Xander walks over to Isabelle and says, "That park there is where I used to feed squirrels sometimes," he points out the window.

She smiles and asks. "Do you think we have time to go over there?"

"Yes, we have plenty of time, but we have to get them some treats," Xander answers. "We can go after they program my phone."

Isabelle smiles.

"Looks like my phone is ready. Let's stop and get some peanuts or something and head over there."

As he slowly walks to the counter to grab his phone.

Isabelle asks, "How much was that phone? It doesn't look like a cheap phone."

"It's not," he answers. "It was 15000 Baht, which is about $500.00, give or take. I will switch my SIM card over when we get home."

"Let's go ahead and get out of here," he says as they walk to the elevator to go down.

12:08 pm Benchasiri Park Sukhumvit Road

"This park is beautiful!" she says as she smiles. "According to the Lonely Planet Book, this park is famous for turtles too."

"I was going to show you the turtles after we feed the squirrels," Xander points off to a group of trees. "In the past, they hung out in this area. Grab your peanuts."

As they walk over to the trees, Isabelle starts to open the bag of peanuts.

"Look," she says as she points to a limb with a white squirrel.

"Now hold up the nut to the edge of the limb, and it should come down," Xander says as he reaches into his back pocket to grab his phone. "I'm going over here to call about our bags."

Now, 4 squirrels have gathered around, each a different color. "Hey, we should have gotten more nuts," she says, looking over and seeing Xander on the phone.

As Xander walks back, he says, "Well, good news and bad news. Good news: they found our bag. Bad news, it's in New York still. It will be here tomorrow evening. Which means it will be 2 days before we get it," he tells Isabelle.

"Well, Shit, That sucks!" She answers back.

Xander says, "Yeah, I know. This is the first time this has happened to me."

"Let's go check out the turtles, then get lunch."

Phrom Phong BTS Station 12:55 pm

Isabelle leans over and asks. "How many stops are we going down?"

"Just one," Xander answers.

"One?" We could have walked that because I can see Asoke Station from here," she says, looking at the BTS map as the train pulls in.

Asoke Station 1:04 pm

As they exit the station and start walking down Sukhumvit Road, Isabelle asks very loudly (traffic, motorbikes, tuk-tuks, cars), "How much further? I'm starving. Remember, I didn't eat on the plane."

"About 5 more minutes," he says.

"Never think about my needs when it comes to food," Isabelle whispers.

9

"Did you say something?" Xander asks.

"Nothing, just thinking to myself," as her stomach growls.

"Here we are. We are turning left here at Soi 10." He tells Isabelle because she is in front of him.

"Taaa Daaa!" As he smiles. Cabbages and Condoms.

"You told me about this restaurant before, and it's got very high reviews," she smiles, looking at the statue made from condoms.

"I have eaten here a few times. They have very good Thai food. It was founded by some doctors from Europe. His team went around in Thailand helping poor villages with Sex Education and HIV treatment." He explains as they walk in.

They quickly sit and order lunch.

"Do you think I can call home?" She asks as the waiter brings out their food.

"Well, it's like 1:30 am at our home. We can do it first thing in the morning. If OK?" he asks.

She smiles as she cuts into her fish.

After lunch, Xander and Isabelle walk back to Sukhumvit to get a taxi to take them back to the Rembrandt Hotel. Xander tells the taxi to wait one moment as they arrive at the hotel.

They get their bags from the hotel.

As they return to the taxi, Xander tells the taxi driver, "Okura Hotel."

"I'm getting tired," she says, her eyes looking heavy.

"Not much longer," he says. "Usually, if there is no traffic, it's about a 10 minute drive."

"Good." She says, "Because this taxi smells horrible."

Okura Hotel 3:16 pm

Isabelle and Xander enter the room on the 10th floor. Isabelle walks over to the windows and looks at the view.

"This view is amazing! Which bed do you want?"

Then Xander says, "Wait until you see the pool. It's on the roof with a vanishing edge."

"Get your bikini, and let's head up," he says as he opens his bag.

"Crap! My shorts are in the other bag. That's OK. I will sit by the pool in my jeans."

Isabelle goes into the bathroom and yells, "Go on up. I will meet you up there."

While sitting by the pool, Xander takes off his t-shirt, orders a cocktail from the waitress, and gets a futon near the pool. Around 15 minutes pass, and Isabelle makes it to the pool area. She walks over, smiles, and puts her robe on the futon. Then jumps into the pool.

Xander stares at Isabelle and thinks to himself, "Wow, she looks great. I haven't seen her body in months."

She leaves the pool and asks, "Can you get me water?"

"Sure," he says as he gets up and heads to the bar.

As Xander comes back from the bar, she says, "I can tell you've been keeping up with your fitness. No more, Dad bod." She laughs.

Xander takes the cap off the water, throws a little water onto Isabelle's stomach, and says, "Eating healthier, working out 2 or 3 times a week if I can."

"Thanks for noticing," he says as he hands her the water.

"What time is it?" She asks.

"I think it's around 4:30 pm," Xander says as he sits back on the futon.

Isabelle lays down in the futon and says, "I'm going to take a nap. I'm still tired from the flight. Can you wake me up in an hour?"

Xander gives her a thumbs up, He lies down and pulls out his phone.

"Excuse me, sir."

"Sir, Sir."

"Excuse me."

Xander wakes up from his nap and notices the waitress next to the futon. "You two have been asleep for a long time. Wanted to see if you were OK?" Waitress asks.

Xander answers, "Yes, we got here yesterday and have jetlag."

Xander looks around and sees Isabelle curl up in a little ball on the futon. He goes by the pool and splashes some water on her face, then notices it's dark outside. Then, he comes back to the futon and grabs his phone.

6.43 pm

"Crap! We overslept," he says to himself.

"Isabelle, Isabelle, babe, hey babe, you need to get up," he says as he gently touches her hand. She softly grabs his hand and pulls it to her chest. He pulls it away and calls her name again. "Isabelle!"

Her eyes open as she sits up with a big yawn. "How long was I asleep?"

"Over 2 hours," Xander answers as he puts on his t-shirt.

"What? 2hrs. I said wake me up in 1hr," she says as an upset look comes over her face.

"Sorry, I fell asleep too," he says as he puts his hand out to help pull her up. "Let's get ready and go get dinner."

"What about our clothes?" she asks. I have 1 pair of shorts, 2 pairs of jeans, and a few t-shirts. "Where are we going? I don't want to be underdressed."

"I know the perfect place, so go ahead and get ready. I need to take care of the bill. I will meet you in the room," he says as he walks towards the bar.

Phloen Chit BTS 8:05 pm

As Isabelle is leaning against the back wall of the BTS train and looking out the window, Xander puts his arm on her shoulder. They both talk as he points to the places where he has been, some of the areas he lived in, and a lot of the new building and how much it has changed. She often points at some of the temples and the different buildings. As he looks at her with a smile.

Phra Khanong BTS 8:31 pm

As they walk down the steps of the BTS, Xander tells her, "It's only a 5 minute walk. We are going to a place called the W district. I lived in this area the last 2 years I was in Bangkok."

She nods her head and says, "It's hard to hear you with all this traffic."

"Understand," he says, grabbing her arm to help guide her through all the people.

After walking for 5 minutes, they turn the corner into the W District as Isabelle pulls her arm away from his hand.

W District is an outdoor food court and market that caters mostly to Thais and foreigners living in Bangkok. Often attracting local artist who can display and sell their art projects and merchandise.

"Isabelle, here is a 1000 Baht. This is more than enough to get some food. I'm going to sit right here and save us this table."

She walks around and checks all the different food stalls. Mostly, it's different types of Thai Food, but she also notices Pizza Oven, Hamburger, and even an Indian Stall. As she walks around, she looks over at Xander, gives him a small smile, and waves. She notices he is writing something.

As she returns with her Shrimp Fried rice with Vegetables, she says, "What are you writing?"

"Just some thoughts and ideas," he says as he gets up to go get himself some food.

Xander returns with Pad Thai and says, "I thought for sure you would get some Indian Food."

"It didn't look good. I ordered some water from the waitress. I need to exchange some money," she says in between her bites.

"Thanks. If you need to exchange a lot, you can do it from an ATM," he says, as he points to an ATM. "Did you tell the bank you were coming here?"

She nods her head.

Moments later, a guitar starts playing, and a girl starts singing. The conversation stops because of the volume. After dinner, Isabelle goes over to the ATM while Xander holds the seats.

She comes back and sits down. "I got 12000 Baht. How much is that in the US?"

"It's around $1000.00," Xander tells her.

"What!" He could tell frustration came over her face.

"I'm kidding. It's about $300," he says as he laughs.

"Ha Ha. Not funny," she says as she softly punches him in his arm.

"Can I use the phone to call my mom? It's 10.00 am there, correct?" She asks.

She grabs the phone and walks over to some Boutique shops to get away from the music. Xander rema ins in his seat and orders a beer. She looks over and sees him writing again. Then she goes back to shopping for clothes.

Xander stops his writing and looks over to check on Isabelle. He could see she was still on the phone while she was still looking at some dresses.

Around half an hour passes by, and she comes back to the table carrying 2 bags.

She hands him back the phone and says, "The phone died; must have run out of minutes. Hard to find clothes to fit."

"Yeah, you're bigger than the average Thai girl," he says as he grabs the phone.

"Bigger?" What are you saying?" She asks.

"Uhhh, sorry, I mean larger or taller," Xander explains, trying to find words to say.

She laughs. "I got you back about the ATM. I'm tired. Are you ready to head back to the hotel?"

"Yes, let's get out of here," he says as he grabs one of her bags.

Chapter 3: Shangri-La

7 am. The alarm on the phone goes off. Xander gets out of bed, looks over, and sees Isabelle already awake.

"Are you ok?" Xander asks.

"Yeah, I'm fine," she says. "It's because back home, it's 7 pm."

Xander gets out of bed and says, "It will take a couple of days to get used to the time difference. Then, have to do it all over again when you get home next week."

"Are you hungry?" he asks as he walks into the bathroom.

"A little," she says as she starts getting dressed.

Xander walks out of the bathroom and says, "We are going to Crepes and Co. French Bakery. It's a short walk from here."

"Sound Lovely. I need a coffee," she says as she opens the door to the room.

Crepes and Co. 7:41 am

"This place is very nice. Did you come here often?" She asks as she opens up the menu.

"No, not often. It was a little far for me just for breakfast," he says, looking at the menu.

"Saweedee Ka! Welcome to Crepes and Co. I'm Long, your waitress."

Isabelle says, "I'd like to have the Banana Crepe with black coffee, please."

"And you, sir?" Long asks.

"I'd like to have the blueberry raspberry crepe. Coffee with cream and sugar and orange juice, please."

"So I've noticed you've been reading the Lonely Planet book. Any places you want to see if we got time?" He asks while sipping on his coffee.

"Kings Palace, some of the Temples, Place called Jim Thompson house. The area called Khaosan Road. Have you been to any of these places?" She asks.

"Our food is here. Let's pray," Xander says as he grabs Isabelle's hand. "Jesus, thank you for the food we are about to eat. Keep us safe as we walk around Bangkok. In your name, Amen."

"I've been to some of these places," Xander says as he takes a bite out of the crepe. "I've been to the Kings Palace but never inside—a couple of the Temples. The older ones made from stone are more interesting. I've never been to the Jim Thompson house. Khaosan Road. I've been a million times. In fact. We will be going there on our trip."

"Yay!" She says as she puts her two index fingers together.

After breakfast, Xander and Isabelle walk back up to Sukhumvit.

Xander points at a department store. "I need to get some clothes."

Isabelle said, "I'm going back to the hotel and sitting by the pool. This is a safe area, right?"

"You will be totally fine," he says. "I should be back in very soon. Be careful."

Xander walks toward the department store next to Chitlom BTS, and Isabelle walks in the other direction toward the hotel.

After Xander returns, they check out of the hotel. Isabelle and Xander board the BTS train to head to the next hotel they are staying at.

"This city is huge," she says.

"I lived here a long time but only saw a fraction of it. Just to go a mile sometimes can take an hour if traffic is bad," he says as he points to the different buildings. "Sky train goes to many more areas now than when I lived here."

Around 30 min go by, and the train stops next to the river. "This is our exit," Xander says as he grabs his bag.

They exit off the BTS station skywalk, which is just a two-minute walk from the back entrance to the Shangri-La hotel.

"This place is so beautiful," she says as they walk through the palm trees and the Flower Garden. "Where did you get the money for this trip?"

He answers, "I had money saved up and using all my credit cards. Also, I got a very good deal this summer on the plane tickets. I wanted to do something special for you for your birthday. This was before we started having problems. Honestly, I didn't think you would go."

"I remember you asking me a question about this. This is around the time my brother went missing," she says as they walk around to the courtyard.

"Doesn't really feel like you're in the city," he says as they sit down next to the pool.

"Let me go see if we can check in yet. Because it's a little past noon and check-in is at 1 pm," Xander says as he walks toward the lobby.

Isabelle walks over to the patio beside the river and sits down in the shade. She orders a coffee and watches all the riverboat traffic: water taxis, Ferry boats, and a barge.

Xander returns and says, "We got our room key. They let us check in 1hr early."

Isabelle: "Great. I got very hot in the sun, and I came over here. It's much cooler next to the river with the breeze."

"How long are we staying here? Because this changing of hotels is getting old," she says.

"We will be here for 2 nights," he says as he sticks his hand out to help her up.

"What are our plans next?" She asks as they are getting into the elevator.

As Xander is pushing the 5th floor, he says, "I was thinking we could go to Lumpini Park. That's the park I pointed to while we were on BTS."

"Sounds good to me," she says as they exit the elevator.

"Afterwards, I wanted to take you to meet my friend and old coach Dominique at his gym," Xander says as they enter the room.

She quickly answers back, "I don't know about the working out part, but you're the tour guide. Besides, I don't have any workout clothes."

Xander looks at her and smiles, "We can get some clothes when we get off BTS as we are going to the park."

Isabelle looks back and just shakes her head.

"Let's go get some lunch at the same area we were, where you were sitting by the river," he says as they both exit the room.

After lunch, Xander and Isabella walk over to BTS. After a short ride, they exit off at Silom BTS.

Silom District 2:05 pm

"Wow! This is a very busy area," she says as she looks up at the tall skyline.

"This way," he says as he taps Isabelle on her shoulder.

Xander points out and explains to Isabelle about Silom. "The gym I used to coach at was on the rooftop of that building," he says as he points down the Soi.

"This is the Japanese Soi. It's the red light district for them," he says as they keep walking. Xander points down another Soi and says, "There are a lot of gay bars at the end of this street. I used to come to this Tapas restaurant on this Soi," he says, as he points at the restaurant.

"Well, I know why you came to this restaurant," Isabella says as she laughs.

"Ha Ha," he says as they keep walking down Silom.

He points down another Soi. "They have a night market here. A few bars and nightclubs, a couple of GoGo bars, and I believe a Ping Pong Show bar around the corner."

As they turned the corner, one of the street vendors had some Thai boxing shorts for sale. After a few minutes of bartering back and forth, he buys them a pair of Thai Boxing shorts and T-shirts.

"We can go across Silom to the department store to pick up a sports bra and a mouthpiece for you," Xander says as he points across the Road.

"No need,'' she says. "I got my bikini top and actually have my mouthpiece."

"Great. Let's head over to the park," he says, grabbing her hand to pull her through the crowd.

They spent around 2 hours walking around and looking at all the nature in the park, feeding the ducks and the Koi fish in some of the ponds. They also notice a monitor lizard sunbathing on the bank.

"We need to get going. I think the class starts at 6 pm." Xander tells Isabelle as they exit the park.

"We will take one of these motorbike taxis," he says. "They can zip through traffic and can get around Bangkok better if there is traffic."

"I'm scared," she says in a concerned voice.

He answers back, "I've never had a problem with one."

They walked over to the motorbike taxis, and Xander tells one of the drivers, "Sukhumvit Soi 11."

Zipping down the road, Xander on the back of one of the motorbikes and Isabelle on another. Weaving in and out of traffic, even driving over the sidewalk. After about a 10-minute ride, they arrive at the corner of Sukhumvit Soi 11.

Xander pays the motorbike taxis and tells Isabelle about the area: "This area is popular for some of the upscale nightclubs, bars, hotels, and condos."

"It has changed a lot since I left," he says as they are walking down the street. "See that hotel on the left? That used to be a little alley. It had several nice restaurants and bars. One of the bars was called Cheap Charlies."

Isabelle is not saying much and just taking everything in.

"Ok, we have arrived," Xander says as he points to The Ambassador Hotel's outside pavilion on the 2nd floor.

"The gym is in a hotel?" She asks.

As they walk through the front plaza into the hotel, Xander says, "I believe it's up this escalator."

At the top of the escalator, they see signs for the kickboxing gym called "The Box."

"I'm going to get my workout clothes on. Wait right here for me. I'm shy," she says as she walks in.

Xander nods his head and says, "No worries."

After both get dressed, they walk into the gym. Isabelle looks over and can tell Xander is looking for his friend.

As one of the fighters comes over and asks, "Can I help you?" in an English accent.

"Where is Dominique?" Xander asks.

Just then, Xander sees Dominique come out of a back room. Dominique looks over and sees Xander and Isabelle.

"Oh my God! My friend!" Dominique says in his French accent. "Seva Bien," as he walks toward Xander.

Dominique and Xander hug and kiss each other on the cheek. Dominique looks over to Isabella and says, "You are more beautiful than the pictures on Facebook." He leans in and kisses her on each cheek.

"Class! Class!" Dominique yells as he introduces them to the gym. "My good friend and a good fighter, Xander, and his beautiful wife, Isabella."

Xander and Isabella's eyes meet for a second, and she gives him an odd look.

Dominique comes over to Isabella and asks, "Would you like to do some sparring with a few of the women fighters?" "I saw you fight before on a video on Facebook."

"Sure," she says as she looks at Xander, "I'm out of shape."

"You will do fine," he says as he sorts through the house gloves and shin pads for her. "I'm going to sit back and coach you for a couple rounds before I work out for myself."

Isabella starts warming up while Xander and Dominique talk.

After about 10 minutes of warming up, Isabella climbs into the ring, looks over at Xander, and winks.

"You got this, Isabella. Out of everyone I have trained, I enjoyed helping you the most and always thought you had great potential," he tells Isabella, giving her the mouthpiece.

Another girl walks over to Isabella and says, "I'm Alessia. Dominique told me to work out with you."

"I'm Isabella." She says as they touch gloves.

DING *DING* *DING* as the bell rings.

Isabella quickly walks over to Alessia and squares off in one of the ring's corners. Isabella attempts to throw a right roundhouse kick to Alessia's leg. Alessia lands a left side kick to Isabella's mid-section, knocking her to the ground. Isabella quickly gets up and moves forward. Alessia steps forward with a jab that lands and shuffles her feet, puts her left leg behind Isabella's right leg, and, with a small shove, sweeps Isabella to the ground. As Isabella got up, Xander could see she was getting frustrated.

Isabella gets to her feet and moves toward Alessia. Isabella fakes a left kick and throws a Superman punch that lands perfectly, knocking Alessia back a little. Isabella moves in before Alessia can get her balance and throws a left and right hook to her head, followed by a left mid-roundhouse kick to the ribs.

"That's it, Izzy!" Xander yells from across the ring.

Alessia and Isabella dance around the ring. Then Alessia throws a right roundhouse kick to Isabella's leg.

"Pop!" As the kick lands.

Isabella steps back from the kick, moves forward, and throws a right roundhouse kick of her own. Alessia shin blocks and returns with a jab that Isabella slips. Then, Izzy slightly leans forward and throws a double right hook—one to the body and one to the head, followed by a left hook to the head. Alessia counters with a push kick, knocking Isabella back a few feet. Alessia comes in for a foot sweep. As Isabella is falling, she grabs Alessia's head and pulls her down with her.

"Izzy, you're doing great; watch your balance with her," Xander tells her.

They both get to their feet, and Isabella throws a double jab, cuts angles to the right, and then throws a left roundhouse kick to the head. Alessia leans back, narrowly missing the kick, and returns with a very hard roundhouse kick to the same leg. Isabella steps back a few feet and shakes her leg out. She gets back to her boxing stance. Alessia moves forward as Isabella throws a jab, steps to the left, and spins around with a left-spinning back fist that lands.

Ding *Ding* *Ding*

"Everyone, take a break," Dominique yells.

Isabella walks over to Xander and says, "She is very good. I can't do another round. I'm exhausted."

Dominique walks over and asks, "One more round?"

"She is too tired," Xander tells Dominique. "She hasn't trained in boxing in over a year."

Alessia walks over to Isabella and hugs her. "You're very good. The other girls here don't do any sparing. Thank you."

"You're welcome."

"Where are you from?" Isabella asks.

"I'm from Italy," Alessia says and turns and walks off.

"Dominique said she has 16 fights," Xander says as he gives Isabella some water.

"I could tell. She is very good with sweeps," Isabella explains to Xander.

"I asked Dominique to work one-on-one with you for a couple of rounds. I'm going to get a workout in for myself," Xander says as he gets his gloves on.

Around 30 minutes pass by, and it's almost 7 pm. Isabella walks over to Xander and tells him, "I'm too tired to keep going, and I'm starting to lose my breath, too."

"You're not looking so good," Xander says as he hands her his water. "You can have the rest of it. You know you always finish my water."

Dominique walks over to Xander and Isabella and says in his French accent, "Oh my friend. How long will you be in Bangkok?" as he puts his arm around Isabella and kisses her on the cheek. "Great girl, Great fighter. Come back and train with us tomorrow."

"We are only here a week, so I don't think we will have time," Xander says as he takes off his gloves. "Let's try to get dinner one night before we go."

"Yes, my friend and I will bring my wife." Dominique smiles and hugs both Isabella and Xander again. He then walks back to the other fighters to start coaching.

"Let's go take a shower and get something to eat," said Xander as he grabbed a towel from the front desk. "Maybe after we eat, we can get a massage."

A giant smile comes over Isabella's face as she walks to the women's dressing room.

7:20 pm

After exiting the Ambassador Hotel and onto the sidewalk of Sukhumvit 11, they decide to cross the street to The Caboose Thai Restaurant since they are both tired and it's closed.

The Caboose is an upscale Thai Restaurant in the heart of the Sukhumvit Soi 11 area. It's an older traditional house with a big garden courtyard and around 15 tables around a little koi pond.

As you walk in the front door, you are greeted with train paraphernalia and a working toy train that circles around the ceiling.

"This place is very nice. I think we might be underdressed for this place," Isabella says as they walk into the courtyard to get a table.

"This is Bangkok. We will be Ok. Plus, I didn't feel like walking far with our stuff," Xander explains.

"Sawadee ka! How many people in your party?" The lady at the front desk asks in a deep voice.

Isabella puts her fingers in the sign 'two.' "Right this way, please," and they follow her to the table, where she gives them their menus.

"Was she a ladyboy?" Isabella asks.

"Yes, I believe she was, but I'm not 100% sure," as Xander takes a drink of water. "Why don't you ask and find out," he says as he laughs.

"Hell to the no!" As she sings out her response. "What do you want to do after we eat?" She pauses to sip some water. "Because I'm still pretty tired."

"I was thinking we get a taxi back to our hotel and go over to the massage shop across the street," Xander says as he looks at the menu.

"It's not one of those Happy Ending massage places, right?" She asks as she laughs.

Xander laughs and says, "It shouldn't be around the Shangri La Hotel. Around this area, it probably would be." He puts his menu down and signals for the waiter.

After dinner, they decided to take a taxi back to the hotel. After a 30-minute taxi ride, they arrive at the hotel at 9:08 pm. They walk straight over to get a massage instead of bringing their bag to the room. As they walk into the shop, they are instantly greeted by the smell of Muscle Balm and Incense. "Welcome, Mr., Welcome Madame," the older Thai women greet Xander and Isabella in their broken Thai English.

"We would like to get 1hr foot massage for both of us, please," As they both sit down in the reclining chairs. Xander pulls out his phone.

"This is the first time you've been on your phone in front of me since we got here. You usually couldn't keep off of it around me," she says sarcastically.

"Well, you used your phone a lot around me, too!" Xander answers back. "Anyways, the message is for you." He hands her the phone and continues, "It's your dad on Instagram."

Isabella grabs the phone and begins messaging her dad. She writes and tells him about the hotels, traveling around on BTS, Lumpini Park, and her workout after about 15 minutes of messaging back and forth. She looks over at Xander to hand the phone back to him and notices he is asleep.

Xander wakes up and notices Isabella looking at photographs on the wall and sipping herbal tea. She notices he is awake and says, "Let's go back to the hotel. I already paid for our massages."

"Thank you. How's everything at home? Your little doggies doing good?" He asks as they exit the door.

After a 3-minute walk, they are back at the hotel. They decide to sit by the river to enjoy the evening and watch some of the boats cruise up and down the river. One is the Dinner Cruises with all their dancing lights. They both hardly spoke a word for 20 minutes.

Xander gets up. "I'm tired. Are you ready to go to bed?" He asks.

"No, I want to be alone. I need some time to myself," she says as she makes herself more comfortable on the futon.

"Ok, well, I might be asleep when you get back," he says as he gets up and grabs both of their bags. "Have a good night."

Xander takes a few steps away, then turns around and comes back to Isabella and says, "I want to say thank you for going on this trip. With what has happened, you could easily have said no. You're the first close friend that has ever come over here with me."

As he takes a few steps backward, she says, "It really means a lot."

Isabella looks at Xander and smiles, and turns back to look at the river.

Chapter 4: Thai Silk

8:00 am, and the alarm sounds on Xander's phone. He opens his eyes and looks over and sees Isabella still asleep in the other bed. "I will let her sleep in for a while," Xander thinks to himself as he gets his clothes on to go downstairs to the café.

"Good morning," Xander says to the waitress at the café bar. "I'd like to have a Caramel Macchiato and a black coffee to go, please."

As he is waiting for his coffee, his phone rings. "Hello"

"This is Etihad Airlines. Your bag came in last night. What hotel are you staying at?" Says the lady on the phone.

"We are at the Shangri La Hotel," Xander answers back while staring at the river traffic from the bar of the café.

"We will send our driver to you with your bag. We apologize for the inconvenience," the lady explains in her Thai accent.

"Thank you," Xander says as he receives his coffee. "Finally, I can stop wearing the same jeans," he mumbles to himself. He grabs the coffee and heads back upstairs.

Xander returns to the room at 8:35 am and sees Isabella still asleep.

"Izzy, Izzy!" He set the coffee on the nightstand next to her bed. "Izzy. I got you coffee." Xander taps her on the shoulder.

"Leave me alone and let me sleep!" She says as she turns away from Xander and pulls the comforter over her head.

"I will go downstairs and sit by the pool," Xander thinks to himself. "She has never been a morning person," he says as he gets up and heads out of the room. A few minutes later, Xander takes a seat by the pool and starts scrolling through his phone, drinking his almost empty Carmel Macchiato. About 1hr passes by, and he returns to the room.

As he enters the room, he hears Isabella singing an old folk song in the shower. "What would you do with a drunken Sailor? What would you do with a drunken Sailor? What would you do with a Drunken Sailor? Early in the morning."

Xander starts singing along. "Way hay and up she raises, way hay and up she raises, Way hay and up she raises, early in the morning. Shave his belly with a rusty razor, Shave his belly with a rusty razor, Shave his belly with a rusty razor."

And before the next chorus, Isabella stops singing.

"Were you singing along with me?" She yells as she turns off the shower.

"I will be out in a few minutes." As she starts humming, something Xander wasn't familiar with.

A few minutes pass, and Isabella comes out of the bathroom with one of the dresses she purchased at the market. "You remember that song?" She asks as she starts braiding her hair.

"You played it all the time when we were in the car together, plus it's a catchy tune," as Xander looks over at her. "Wow! You look very lovely in that dress," he says as he smiles. "Oh, good news, too. Our bag came in, and they will be bringing it here."

"Thank you, and thank you for the coffee," she says as she is still working on her hair. "Awesome, be glad to get the rest of my stuff," she says as she finishes her hair. "What are our plans today?"

"Well, I figure we can hang out around here for a while. I believe our bag is en route," he says as he looks for something clean to put on. "How late did you stay out last night?"

"I think I got back to the room around 1 am," she said as she walks back into the bathroom. "You know me. I like my alone time to think." She walks back out with her makeup bag. "I ordered a glass of wine from the bar and just relaxed," as she tosses the bag on the bed. "A guy from Australia came up to me while I was at the bar. We talked for about 15 minutes."

"Really?" he asks, as a small smile comes to his face. "Well, you are a beautiful lady! What did you guys talk about?" He asks.

Isabella bends over and starts putting on her shoes. "Well, he did most of the talking. He is here with his wife on their 16th Wedding Anniversary," as she raises up, "Older guy. I believe he said he was 61."

"Where was his wife?" Xander says as he goes into the bathroom.

"He told me his wife went to bed early, and he wanted to sit by the river and have a glass of wine," she explains while checking herself out in the mirror. "The guy kind of reminded me of you a little."

"Oh yeah! How's that?" As he walks out of the bathroom, he says, and notices Isabella spinning around while looking at herself in the mirror. "What are you doing?" He asks.

She stops and looks at Xander, "I'm checking out my butt. Seeing if it looks good in this dress." Then she starts to explain, "Well, the guy was very talkative and outgoing. It didn't seem he wanted to listen to much of what I wanted to say. But you know I don't talk much to strangers. And he said he used to do Judo," she says as she spins around one more time, "Oh, and his wife was 39."

"Hey, I listen to you," Xander says with a concerned look. "Well, sorry if you felt that way. You often wanted alone time or wanted to read."

"Let's not talk about the past; we both agreed not to do that for this trip, remember," said Isabella as she was unbraiding her hair.

"You're right; you're right. Sorry," says Xander. "You know I like you in your braids," he says as he looks to see which shirt is the cleanest.

"It makes my hair curlier," she explains as she finishes taking out the last braid. "But I usually got to keep it in all night. What's our plan today?"

"I was thinking we could go to the Jim Thompson house if our bag gets here soon. If not, I need to go shopping. My shirts smell horrible," he says, as he starts squirting his shirt with cologne. Well, let's head downstairs and get brunch.

10:07am Café at Shangri La Hotel

As Xander and Isabella are having brunch at the café, one of the concierges brings them information about the Jim Thompson house. While they are looking at the brochure at the Jim Thompson house, they start planning their afternoon. After brunch, Xander goes to the front desk to check to see if their bag has been delivered. As he looks over the counter, he notices their bag. "Yes !!!!" He says as he thinks to himself. He returns to the café, bag in hand. He sees Isabelle do her little index finger touching.

"I'm going to put on some clean clothes," says Xander as he motions for the bill.

"I'm ready to go," Isabella says as she sips on her coffee. "I will wait here for you."

Xander smiles and heads up to the room to change. Around 15 minutes pass by, and Xander returns to the café. After talking for a few minutes, they start walking to the BTS Station.

11:16 am National Stadium BTS

Xander and Isabella arrived at National Stadium BTS. They walk over to the handrail so they could get a better look at the area. Xander points over to the right toward the arena. "This is the National Stadium. This is where I trained with the Thai National Judo Team before they moved location." He points to the mall just to their left. "This is MBK Mall; it's a good place to shop for Thai t-shirts and souvenirs instead of outside markets." Then, Isabella and Xander head down to the skywalk to cross over to the other side. They both stop at the handrail and Xander points to the right. "This is Siam Discover," and then points down even further. "That is Siam Paragon."

"This place is nothing more than a big mall," she says as she leans over the handrail to get a better look.

"Siam Paragon is the mall that had the exotic car dealership inside. It was one of my favorite malls. It also has a giant Aquarium inside, like the one we went to in Gatlinburg," Xander explains, and then turns and points to his left. "Jim Thompson House is about a 5-minute walk that way off a side street."

"I'm thirsty," Isabella says as they turn to walk down the stairs to the main road. "It's very hot today. I don't want to have a heat stroke while I'm here. My mom would kill you!"

"Look! A fruit vendor!" Xander says as he points to a cart full of pineapples and coconuts in an ice chest. "How about ice-cold fresh coconut water?"

"You're my hero," as she smiles.

They order two coconuts, and the vendor pulls them out of the ice chest. He gets a meat cleaver and puts the coconut in the palm of his hand. He makes a few slices with the cleaver as he is spinning it like a basketball in his palm. Plucks in the straw. Gives it to Isabella and proceeds to do the same for Xander.

"This is so good!" she says as she smiles. "I can see why you got these all the time."

"It's really hot. How much further?" She says as her smile leaves her face. "You said 5 minutes, 5 minutes ago."

"Actually, we are standing at the entrance of the soi now." Xander points down the street. "According to the map. It's just a few buildings down."

"Great, because I'm ready to get out of the sun," she says as she takes another sip from the coconut.

11:37 am Jim Thompson House

Xander and Isabella arrive at a red stone wall outside of Jim Thompson House. They walk up to inquire about a tour.

"Tickets available for the next guided tour start at 12:30 pm," said the lady behind the ticket booth to everyone who had gathered around. Xander quickly joins in the line to get them the tickets.

"What do you think of this place so far?" Xander asked as he handed the ticket to Isabella.

"This place is beautiful," she says in excitement. "You know how I like Mansion tours," she continues as she looks at one of the huge trees in the garden. "I'm surprised you have never been here before."

"Don't seem like you're in Bangkok," Xander says as he admires the traditional Red Thai Teak house. "This is beautiful craftsmanship," he continues as he knocks on one of the huge wood columns. "Just think, at one time, there were probably all kinds of houses like this in Bangkok." They start walking around the courtyard.

Isabella bends over to smell some flowers she has never seen before. "I definitely could live in this house. Oh look, they have plumbing and electricity, too," she says jokingly.

Xander ignores the remark as he stops to take a picture on his phone. "Izzy, Come over here. Check out this little pond they got here," as he points down at some of the fish.

"Can we keep walking around here, or is this for the tour?" Isabella asks as she comes over to look at the pond.

"I guess I don't see any signs," Xander responds. "Let's walk over here to the gift shop."

"These silks are *hardd*," Isabella responds in Welsh as she looks through the patterns. "Do you think I should get my mom a scarf or pillowcase?"

"Yes, these silks are beautiful," Xander responds. "Why not just get both?"

"You understood my Welsh?" As she turns and looks at Xander.

"I studied a little this winter during the snowstorm we had." He says as he points to a pillowcase and smiles.

She smiles back. "I'm going to get the pillowcases for her couch and this scarf here." As she starts looking around and continues, "I need to find something for my dad."

"I can't see your dad wearing a silk scarf." As Xander laughs, "Our tour is about to begin."

As they get ready to enter the house, the tour guide instructs them to take off their shoes. As the tour begins, she tells them some of the history of the house and about Jim Thompson. The inside of the house is full of mostly traditional Thai wood furniture and a few Western pieces. The tour lasts for about 1 hour, and they come back to the front to collect their shoes.

"I really enjoyed this place," Isabella says as she looks through the pictures on her phone. "What do you want to do next?"

"Are you hungry?" He asks.

"Does a bear shit in the woods?" As she laughs.

Xander laughs back. "How about some Thai street food?"

"As long as it's safe," she answers.

As they walk out of the Jim Thompson house, they notice a motorbike with a food vendor trailer attached to it. There are four folding tables and a few chairs.

"How about some soup?" Xander says as he sees what they have.

"As long as it doesn't have meat in it," she responds as she sits down at one of the tables.

"How about fish sausage, or you can get it plain with just vegetables," Xander says as he points to the chicken for himself.

"I will try the fish," she says as she turns and looks at a street dog that came up to her. "Ah, this guy is cute," she says as she starts to pet him. "He looks injured." Suddenly, more dogs come over to the table. "There are a lot of stray dogs in Bangkok."

He brings back the soups to the table and sits down. "Let's pray," he says as they grab each other's hand. "Jesus, thank you for the food we are about to eat. Keep us safe today as we tour Bangkok. Amen." Xander slides a spoon over to Isabella. "If you don't like the fish. Just throw it to the ground. These stray dogs will usually eat it," he says as he adds some chili pepper vinegar to his soup.

Isabella starts to pour some water onto her hands to clean them off and says, "After we eat, what's our plan?" Then, she adds a spoonful of chilies to her soup.

"Well, I was thinking we could head back to the hotel and hang out by the pool and relax for a while," he answers as he throws a small piece of chicken to the dog she was petting earlier. "Or would you like to try indoor surfing at a wave pool?"

"Surfing!" A smile lights up the shaded street.

After heading back to the hotel to get extra clothes and to drop off their goods from Jim Thompson's house, they walk down to hail a taxi.

4:13 pm Sukhumvit Soi 26 Flow House

"This area looks totally different than the other parts of Bangkok," Izzy says as she steps out of the taxi. "Most everywhere you go in Bangkok, either it's inside a big mall or near these high rises."

"Yep! I agree," Xander said after paying for the taxi. "This area is a few blocks away from Sukhumvit. A lot of nice houses around here. The developers have a harder time buying the property up around here. So it has kept some of its older charm. Well, here we are." He points to Flow House.

"The entrance kind of looks like your cabin with the board and batten," she says as they walk to the entrance. "Or an old beach cabin you see in Florida."

"I think that's the look they were going for here. This place was built like in 2014 or something," Xander says as they arrive at the entrance.

Xander buys two surfing passes; they go inside and walk up to the surfing area. Bob Marley was playing on the speakers, and there was also the sound of roaring water. Isabella can't keep from smiling.

"I'm going to change and put my swimming trunks on," he says as he grabs his shorts. He turns around and can see Isabella already taking her dress off.

"I put my bikini on while we were at the hotel." She looks over and smiles. "Rydw i'n mynd I aros yma," she says in Welsh.

"Sorry, what did you say?" He asks. "I think you were speaking in Welsh?"

She answers, "I'm going to wait here."

"Ok, be right back," he says as he walks off.

5 min later, Xander comes back to the area where he left Isabella, and she is gone. He looks over to the bar and through the crowds of people sitting down. Then he hears his name from a distance.

"Xander! Xander! look behind you!" She yells from the stairs of the surfing area. "The line to use the surf area was getting long."

Xander gives her a thumbs up as he proceeds to queue in line.

She looks down at Xander, gives him a small wave and smile, and then turns around to watch the next rider.

"One more rider, then it's Isabella's turn," he thinks to himself.

The 5-minute timer goes off to signal the end of the turn. Isabella is up next. She straps the leash of the board to her wrist. She looks at the lifeguard, gives him a thumbs up, looks down at Xander, and gives him the middle finger. Xander just laughs as he shakes his head.

The timer starts, and Isabella grabs the board and holds it firmly to her chest. She slightly bends over and then leaps onto the surf ramp. Gravity pulls her down close to the bottom of the ramp. She then arches her back and slightly pulls the front of the board up, and she glides into the middle of the ramp. She pulls her left side up and drifts right; she then pulls her right side up and drifts left.

"You're doing great, Izzy!" Xander yells from the steps, "See if you can get on one knee."

Isabella looks at the lifeguard as he motions for her to get on her knees. She nods her head, straightens her arms out, and then slides her knees to her chest. Then, suddenly, the board flies out from under her, and water pressure pushes her to the top of the ramp. She hops up, adjusts her bikini top, and grabs the board to try again. Running with the board and in a diving motion, she leaps onto the surf ramp and immediately loses her balance. The water pushes her back to the top surface. She gets up and looks down at Xander.

"Do what you did the first time," he yells.

She nods her head, grabs the board firmly to her chest, and leaps onto the ramp. After a few seconds, she straightens her arms and pulls her knees to her chest. She slides left then right across the ramp, and she notices the lifeguard signaling to her to get to one foot. She leans a little to her right and slams into the wall but remains on the board. Isabella then leans to the left and brings the board to the center. She leans on her right again and quickly brings her left foot to the board. The lifeguard at the bottom of the ramp signals her to stand up. Isabella nods her head, slides her right leg down a little, pushes off with her arms, and plants her right leg.

"You're up, you're up!" Xander yells in amazement.

Isabella slowly tries to stand up even further and loses her balance. She crashes onto the ramp. At that moment, her bikini top flies off as she gets pushed to the top of the ramp. She quickly gets to her knees and puts her arms over her breast. The lifeguard springs into action, takes his towel, and throws it at Isabella. She grabs the towel, wraps it around herself, and then finds her top. Isabella can see people smiling and laughing. She quickly heads down the exit stairs.

Xander hops out of line and sprints over to her. "You gave everyone a nice show there," he says in laughter.

"Oh my God, that was so embarrassing!" She says as she starts to cry.

"Come here." Xander puts his arms around her and gives her a hug. "You did awesome, by the way."

"Thank you," she says as she wipes a tear from her face. "I need to go put my top on."

"I will wait right here for you, babe," Xander says as he points to a bench next to him.

As Isabella comes out of the locker room, Xander hands her his t-shirt and says, "I thought you would need this if you tried it again."

"Thanks!" She says as she reaches up to grab the shirt. "Now I see why half the girls here have t-shirts on."

Xander smiles. "I'm sure this happens all the time. I'm going to hop back in line."

"Wait, I will come with you," she says as she smiles.

Xander and Isabella surfed a few more times. Then, they agreed they had enough. Both head to the locker rooms to shower and get dressed.

Xander is the first one to be ready as he waits patiently for Isabella to get out. He looks at himself in the mirror as he tries to get a cowlick to lie down. Isabella comes out of the locker room wearing a different dress than earlier. "Is that one of your new dresses?" He asks.

"Yes, what do you think?" She answers back.

"Yes, the dress looks very good on you."

"Where are we going to eat?" She says as she starts to mess with Xander Cowlick. "I assume somewhere nice because you are looking handsome.

"Thank you," he says as he turns toward the exit.

"Hello? Don't ignore me." Isabella says as he turns his back on her.

"Sorry, I wasn't intentionally trying to ignore you." As he turns back around, he says, "My neck hurts a little when I fell up against the wall early."

"You can at least acknowledge me," she says, then laughs. "Yeah, you're always hurting yourself."

"The name of the place we are going to is Wine Connection," he says as they are walking through the parking lot. "It's a very long walk."

"I hope it's not a long walk. It's very humid tonight," she mentions as she slows down and asks, "Can we get a taxi?"

"Let's get out of the parking lot and walk up to Sukhumvit 26 first," he says as he starts to laugh.

"What's so funny?" She asks as they approach Sukhumvit 26. "Why, you got to be kidding me all the time?" Then she notices the sign (Wine Connection) across the street.

7:16 pm K Village Food Mall

As they walk across the street into K Village, they immediately go to Wine Connection and ask for a table.

"You want to sit outside or inside," Xander asks. "The sun is going down, and it will cool off quickly."

"Let's sit outside," said Isabella as she starts looking at the wine list. "This place reminds me of the food hall we went to a few times in downtown Nashville, except it's at street level."

"Yes, it's very similar. They also have a grocery store over there and a few places to shop. But 50% of the place is restaurants," he says as they start following their hostess.

"It's got a nice atmosphere," she says as she sits down and grabs the menu. "Nice change because I was tired of eating Thai food. You want to order some wine?" She asks.

"How about this bottle here from Australia? It's a Moscato," Xander says as he starts to look at the appetizer on the menu. "And let's get a Charcuterie board."

"I was just thinking the same thing," she exclaims as she smiles.

Moments later, the waitress brings out a loaf of bread and asks. "Welcome, I'm Porn. Can I start you off with an appetizer and some wine?

"I would like to have a bottle of the Jacobs Creek Moscato and the Charcuterie Board, please," Xander says as he points at the Charcuterie Board on the menu.

"I already know what I want for dinner," Iseballa tells the waitress. "I like to have the smoked salmon with broccoli and cauliflower."

"And you, sir?" Porn asks.

"I will have the 6oz sirloin with vegetable medley," he says as he hands the waitress back the menu.

They spend the next 1 hour and a half reminiscing while enjoying their food. Isabella often got her phone out and edited some of the pictures while they were having dinner. "I think you spend more time on your phone now than I do." Xander laughs.

"When I get back to the hotel, I can connect with the Wi-Fi and post some pictures. And I was going over my work schedule for next week when I get back home," she says as she finishes her glass of wine. "What's our plan after this?"

"I was thinking we can walk around here for a little while and, afterward, go to Sukhumvit 11." He motions for the check.

"Sukhumvit 11, is that where we went yesterday and trained?" She asks.

"There is a sports bar there called the Australian Bar. They had a very good band in the past," he replies as he stands up to get his wallet out.

"What kind of music?" she says as she puts her phone away.

As he gives money to the waitress, he answers, "They play music like the Foo Fighters, Green Day, Kings of Leon. Things like that."

"Sounds good," she says as she stands up. "I think I'm a little tipsy," as she laughs.

They leave Wine Connection and walk around K Village as they continue to talk. They stop at the Apple Store, a dog apparel store, and a few other shops and then sit down next to the fountain.

"You ready to get a taxi and head out of here?" he says as he stands up. She just nods her head. "Are you Ok? He asks.

"Yeah, I just want to be quiet for a little while," she says as she stands up.

They both walk to Soi 26 to hail a taxi to Sukhumvit Soi 11. Isabella spent most of the time just staring out the window. "Are you Ok?" Xander asks again.

"Yes! I just want to be quiet," she responds and keeps looking out the window.

9:37 pm Australian Bar

Xander and Isabella exit out of the taxi and proceed to walk up the stairs to the entrance of the bar. The band is already playing, and a few women are dancing on the dance floor. They look around to find an empty table and chairs. They finally spot a high top off to the corner of the room next to the stage. Isabella sits down and looks at the Australian memorabilia displayed on the walls.

"This place is packed," she says as she looks up at a stuffed crocodile mounted to the wall. "This band is really good," she says as she moves her head with the music.

"The band is from the Philippines. Do you want anything to drink?" Xander asks.

"Naa, I'm good at the moment." She starts livening up and stands. "I think if I sit down at the moment, it will make me sleepy," she says as she looks over at the next table with 3 Thai ladies sitting down.

"Hey, Xander!" She yells. "Let's get a fishbowl." As she points at the girl's drink next to them.

Xander nods yes and signals to the waitress.

Isabella looks over at Xander, who is talking to the waitress and sits back down.

"Hey, I'm going to the bathroom," he says as he leans over and shouts at Isabella. She gives him a thumbs up.

As he walks back to the table, he notices Isabella is gone. He sits down and looks around and sees she is dancing with some of the Thai girls who are sitting next to them. She looks over toward him and motions for him to join them. He puts his index finger in the air, signaling one moment just as the waitress brings their fishbowl. He takes a sip and walks over to Isabella.

"These girls said I look like Jennifer Lawrence, and they thought I had a nice butt," she yells while dancing. "Here, dance with this one," she grabs Xander's hand and pulls him closer to the Thai girls.

Xander resists and comments back, "I'm going to sit back down; I don't like this song." He goes back to the table to sit down.

Isabella follows him back and sits down. "Thanks for the drink," she says as she takes a sip. "Are you having a good time tonight?

"What?" Xander shouts back.

Isabella leans over to Xander's ear. "Are you having fun?" She shouts.

"Yes, not bad," Xander answers as he grabs the fishbowl.

The band starts to play Nirvana (In Bloom). Xander and Isabella both look at each other in excitement. Just then, the Thai girls sitting next to them pull them onto the dance floor. Xander and Isabella looked at each other while singing the song. Their heads go side to side and back and forth. The song tempo picks up, and they both start bouncing up and down. "This band sounds just as good as that tribute band we went to see," Isabella screams into his ear.

He just smiles as the Thai girls join in on their singing. As the song closes, Isabella goes over to get another drink.

Moments pause as the song ends. And the lead singer asks the crowd. "You want to hear one more Nirvana song?"

As the next song started to play, Isabella and Xander sang along as loud as they could, "I'm so happy,". Xander and Isabella start to jump up and down. They turn, look at each other, and yell, "Yeah, yeah!"

The songs end, and Isabella and Xander walk back to take a drink. Ban plays the next song. Kings of Leon (Your Sex is on Fire). Isabella jumps up. "I love this song," she yells as she grabs Xander's hand to pull him back out to dance. They get very close, and their hips move back and forth like you would see in salsa dancing. Isabella slightly pushes Xander away, turns around, and starts dancing by herself. She leans back and says in his ear, "Dance with one of the girls that are sitting next to us." Then, she grabs one of the Thai girls' hands and pulls her over to Xander.

After the song, they sit back down. "You should talk to the girl you were dancing with." She says as she finishes the last of the fishbowl. "She is cute."

"I'm OK," he says as he nods. "Hey, I'm going to go to the bathroom. Please stay right here. I think maybe you have drunk too much."

Xander comes back from the bathroom and sees Isabella's head on the table with one of the Thai girls rubbing her neck. "What happened?" He asks one of the girls.

"We look over and see her head down. Don't know? Mea Mi (Thai for drunk or not)," the girl says.

Isabella raises up and says, "Khop Khun Kah. (Thai for thank you)" to the Thai girl. "Xander, can we go back to the hotel?"

"Yes, it's not a problem. We must get early tomorrow anyways." Xander answers back.

Isabella gives the girls a hug and grabs Xander's arm for support as they start to walk out of the bar. Xander hails a taxi and then proceeds to help Isabella get into the taxi. They arrive back at the hotel a little after 11 pm. Xander helps Isabella back to the room.

"Can you help me to the bathroom?" Isabella asks Xander.

"Are you really that drunk?" Xander answers back.

"You know it doesn't take much for me to get drunk," she responds as she laughs.

Xander helps her to the bathroom and gets her some water. "Do you want to take a hot shower?" He asks.

"No. I just need to go pee," she sighs.

After a few minutes, Isabella comes out of the bathroom and gets into her bed with her dress still on.

Xander gives her a grin and tells her, "Good night."

Chapter 5: Sand in my shoes

6:00 am and the alarm rings on Xander's phone. He looks at his phone and pushes the snooze. "10 more minutes," he thinks to himself. 6:10 am, the alarm rings again. Xander slowly rolls out of bed and walks to the bathroom. He looks over at Isabella. She is lying crossways in the bed. One of her legs is hanging off the side of the bed. Xander just laughs as he starts to tickle her foot. She jumps and pulls her legs together. "Izzy, Izzy." Xander gently taps her on the leg. "Hey, we have a busy day. Get up. Please," he tells her.

"Mmmm," she says as her eyes open. "Can you get me some water?" She asks, "What time is it?"

"It's a little after 6:00 am," he answers, as he walks into the bathroom to shower.

After the shower, he comes out of the bathroom, and Isabella is already up. "You never told me what we are doing today?" She asks as she looks for something to wear.

"It's a surprise, but I'm sure you will love it." He smiles as he starts to pack his clothes. "Please hurry up and get ready." Xander looks at the time on his phone. "We need to check out of the room."

"OK, OK, it would be better if you tell me what you are doing," she says as she proceeds to the bathroom.

"You will see," he answers.

6:48am Taxi at the Shangri-La

Xander and Isabella take a seat in the taxi. Xander hands the driver a note written in Thai. It reads, "Sabia Lodge Pattaya Beach. I wanted to surprise my friend by taking her to the beach. Please don't say out loud, Pattaya."

"OK, Krap," the taxi driver says. "3000 baht ok?" He asks.

"3000 baht?!" She utters in a surprised manner. "Most of our fairs are around 100. How long of a ride is it?" She asks.

"I think it's around 1 hour and a half, maybe 2 hours. I don't remember," Xander replies as he pulls his phone out to look at different tours in Pattaya.

"OK, well, I will go back to sleep," she says as she makes herself comfortable. "You know I have car Narcolepsy," she exclaims as she closes her eyes.

9:02 Pattaya

The taxi pulls off the main road and turns into an alley. Xander gently taps Isabella on her side, who is now using his leg as a pillow. "Hey, wake up; we are almost here."

Isabella rises up, gives a big yawn, and asks how much further.

"I'm not sure, but I think we are close because the taxi just pulled off the main road," he answers back.

Isabella starts staring out the windows and utters. "Looks like we are still in Bangkok. All I see is tall buildings around us." As she turns and looks out the windshield. "Is that the beach?" She asks as she suddenly wakes up.

"Yep," he answers back with a big smile.

"Before we left, you said we didn't have time for the beach because we are only here for a week," she explains in excitement.

"Well, surprise!" He says as he continues to smile.

The taxi pulls up to the front of the hotel. "We are here," the taxi driver says. They both get out of the taxi and head inside to the lobby. Isabella gets her Lonely Planet Book and starts to read as Xander checks in.

Xander walks back to Isabella. "Here is your room key."

"Room key?" She asks, surprised.

"They didn't have two beds in a room. So, I got you your own private room," he says as he grabs their bags and starts walking toward the elevator. "Go check into your room, get your bikini and a towel, and meet me back here in 15 mins. I have another surprise!" He says with a grin.

15 mins later, they meet back at the lobby and then proceed to go outside to the alley. "We must wait here for our ride. They are supposed to be here at 10 am," Xander says as he removes his t-shirt.

"When I was reading the Lonely Planet Book, it says Pattaya is the prostitution capital of Thailand," she says in a concerned voice.

"Yes, it's very open here in Pattaya," he responds with a grin, "but it's not everywhere, and there are a lot of family things to do here as well." As he starts to point to a truck with a camper top on it. "I think our ride is here."

"We are riding in the back of a truck?" She asks. Then, she reads the logo on the side of the door. Pattaya Scuba Adventures. "We are going scuba diving?" As she slightly jumps up and down.

"No. We are going snorkeling," says Xander as he grabs their bag with the towels.

Xander and Isabella climb into the back of the truck and sit down on one of the benches. They are greeted by some other couples in the back that were already seated. Just then, the truck slowly takes off and drives to another hotel to pick up the last diver. As they reach the pier, the time is a little after 11 am. Everyone climbs out of the truck as they follow the staff to the boat.

"Have you done this before?" Xander asks as they sit down in the boat.

"Yes. I think I told you I did it before when I lived in Florida," she replies as she takes a sip of water. "I didn't have any coffee, and I'm hungry," she says as she looks at him and says, "You haven't changed."

"What?" Xander asks as he looks at her back.

"I don't matter now," she says as she turns to look at the instructor. "They are about to talk about ship safety."

The instructor begins his safety speech and things to look out for during the cruise. After the ship safety speech, he yells, "First stop is Ko Sak Island, where they will have lunch ready for you," in his Thai British accent. "And we have fresh coffee and drinks at the rear of the boat." He then gives the signal for the Captain to (make way.)

"Well, I must admit. He did do a good job planning this day out after all," she thinks to herself as she turns back to look at Xander. "Can you get me a coffee, please?" She asks.

The boats arrive at the island around 30 minutes later and drop anchor 30 feet from shore. One of the staff members instructs all the guests about the island: "You can either swim ashore or you can board our little lifeboat," as he points to the rear. "We will be here for 1hr 30mins. Feel free to snorkel around while we prepare lunch," he announces as he points to an area off the port side of the boat. "This area has a small coral reef where you can see many pretty fish. Please don't touch the coral because it can kill the coral." "Enjoy!"

They both grab their snorkel, face mask, flippers, and life jacket and start heading to the Aft of the boat.

Isabella jumps off the side, then yells, "Come on old man. Jump in."

Xander leaps into the water and responds back, "This water is very warm." As he swims over to Isabella, he says, "Let's swim over to the coral he was talking about."

Xander and Isabella swim over to the coral and take off their life vest. They take a deep breath and dive down around 10ft under the water, close to the reef. They see several little fish swimming in and out of the coral. They come back to the surface for some air and dive back down again. Isabella taps Xander on the arm and points to a crab moving along in the sand. They surface to grab their life vest and swim along, looking at the bottom while breathing through the snorkel. 45 mins go by, and they swim ashore.

"There is not a lot of fish here," Isabella says as she gets in line to get lunch.

"This area is overfished, and I guess all the tourists here don't help," he explains as he gets his plate. "But did you have fun?" He asks.

"Yes, I really enjoyed it," she responded as they sat down with their lunch. "What's our plan tonight?" She asks as they lower their heads to pray.

"Well, I was thinking we could walk along the board walk on the beach and get dinner," he answers and then takes a bite of food and pauses for a second, "I'm not sure what they have here for restaurants."

Isabella swallows and responds, "I'm good with that. "I don't think I want to stay out late because of last night." As she wipes her mouth. "I didn't get enough sleep."

Xander takes another bite, and, finishing chewing, he says, "Looks like a storm in the distance," as he points to the south.

"I've noticed you don't talk as much with food in your mouth," she says as she turns to look where he is pointing. "I hope it doesn't come this way."

"I know you complain about that often, and it's a bad habit. So, I try to be mindful of that now when eating." Xander then stands up, grabs their paper plates, and throws them into the trash can.

They board the boat to finish the rest of the cruise. The boat goes around ½ mile from Ko Sak and drops anchor again. "This is another coral reef. We will be here for 30 mins then back to port," one of the staff explains. All the tourists prepare to go snorkeling one more time before heading back in. After arriving back on land, Xander and Isabella look for a taxi back to the hotel.

4:37 pm Sabia Lodge Hotel

Isabella and Xander arrive back at the hotel and discuss the agenda for the evening. They agree to meet back at the lobby in 1 hr. Isabella arrives at the lobby and can see Xander sitting by the pool writing something. She walks out to meet him to discuss the evening.

"What are you writing?" She asks.

"Just some random thoughts," he answers as he stands up. "You're looking cute."

"I never saw you taking notes before other than something for work," she says as they make their way out into the street. "So, what's our plan this evening?" She asks again.

"Well, if it doesn't rain. I was hoping we could just walk down the beach and then get dinner and just decide then," he answers.

After walking for a few minutes, they arrive at Beach Road. They cross the street to the sidewalk along the beach. The sun is already starting to set, and the storm is getting closer. Sounds of sea birds, waves crashing on the beach, and thunder in the distance set the mood for a relaxing and possibly romantic evening. As they walk along, they are often greeted by merchants on the beach. "Welcome, have a look" is the most common phrase. They look out on the beach and see the jet ski rentals being pulled off the beach and the beach merchants folding up all the beach umbrellas.

After walking for around 15 mins, they feel it lightly sprinkling. "I think it is going to storm here soon. We need to get off the beach," Xander says as he points across the street. "Hey, let's go into Harbor Mall."

"Sounds good because I don't want to get rained on," she says as she starts to laugh. "You know I don't wear a bra often. I will be giving everyone a show in this white dress."

Xander laughs and comments, "You don't want to give everyone a show again?"

Just as they cross the street, the rain picks up, and they run into the mall. They walk up to the information desk to see its directory. Isabella starts reading off things to do inside the mall: "They have a movie theater on the top floor. A bowling alley, an arcade, and an ice-skating rink."

"Too bad they don't have an escape room. Remember the escape from prison one we did?" He asks.

"Yeah, I remember," she answers, and she continues to read the directory to herself. "We did that one in Gatlinburg last Christmas," she says as she turns and looks at Xander and smiles. "We almost got out! You want to go ice skating?" She asks.

"I'm down for that," he says as they turn and start walking in the direction of the rink. "Sounds like it's getting bad outside," as they both can hear the wind and rain hitting the windows and the roof.

6:43 pm The Rink Harbor Mall

As they walk inside the door, they are greeted suddenly with a temperature change. Isabella looks at Xander and questions, "Maybe this wasn't a good idea. Might be too cold."

As both look out into the rink, they see some skaters wearing jackets and sweaters and a few people wearing t-shirts. They sit down in the hockey bleacher to see how cold it gets next to the rink.

"After about 10 mins," Xander says, "I think we will be OK. Let's go get our skates."

"Hey, I got a white dress on. What if I fall?" She asks.

"I think people fall down all the time out here," he answers as he grabs his skates.

"Hello! White dress, Ice, Ice is made from water," she explains as she sits down with her skates.

"They have long-sleeved t-shirts for sale. I will get one for both of us," Xander says as he heads back to the counter.

As they lace up their skates and walk onto the ice, Isabella quickly skates away and makes a turn to see where Xander is. She notices him getting up from a fall and skates back to him. "Are you OK?" She asks as she laughs.

"Yes, I'm fine. Give me a min or so, and I should catch on," he replies as he pushes off slowly. "When I was in my early 20s, I went rollerblading all the time," he says as he catches back up to Isabella.

Occasionally, one of them falls, and the other gives a hand to pull the fallen person up. Isabella must be mindful of her dress when falling. Xander, being a good friend, would quickly turn around to give a hand. No mention of the past, just two old friends having a great time. After an hour of skating, Isabella is getting cold.

"I'm starting to get cold, and my ass is a little wet," Izzy says as they exit off the ice rink. Isabella turns around and tries to look at her butt. "Can you see through my dress?" "It's a little wet." She asks.

"You're good," Xander says, and he sits down to take off the skates. "You want to get something to eat?"

"Sounds good to me. I think it might be raining still," she says as she grabs her skates. "When I was looking at the directory early. There are a lot of restaurants here."

They return the skates and exit out into the concourse to find a directory map. They can still hear the rain on the roof and wind howling. "You want to get sushi?" Xander asks as he sees a Japanese restaurant from a distance.

After dinner, they walk to the ground floor but can see it is still raining out the window. Xander turns around and says to Isabella, "I think we might have to walk. The mall is closing soon, and it's impossible to get a taxi," as he points to a sporting goods store. "They might have a rain jacket or something for us."

"You're the man; go get something for us," she suggests as she looks at Xander with a look of concern. "Can I use your phone? I want to call my mom."

"Sorry, I didn't know it was going to rain," he answers as he hands her the phone. "I will be right back."

After returning from the store, he saw Isabella sitting on a bench, still talking with her mom. "Tell your mom hello and that I love her."

Isabella looks at Xander, nods her head, and says to her mom, "Xander said hello and that he loves you guys." She then puts the phone on speaker.

"Hey! Xander. Isabella said you guys are having a good time," Isabella's mom says on the phone. "Well, I know this phone call cost a lot of money. Miss you and love you both."

Isabella hands the phone back to Xander and asks, "So, did you find us something?"

"Yes, I got us ponchos," Xander replies as he hands one of the ponchos to her.

"What's our plan now?" She asks as she puts the poncho on.

"This rain kind of messed up my plans for the evening," he answers as he puts his poncho on. "I wanted to go to Walking Street, but I don't feel like doing that in this rain." "I guess head back to the hotel."

"Yeah, I'm OK with that," she says as they walk out into the rain. "I'm a little tired from last night anyway."

They walk out of the mall's plaza and back onto Beach Road. Their hotel is only a 15 min walk from the mall. As they are walking along the sidewalk on Beach Road, the sound is deafening. Music is playing from the many bars along the street. Thai girls working at the bars yelling at men, "Welcome" and "Sexy Man," as they pass by. Cars splashing water on the road and rain falling on the metal roofs.

Isabella leans in and yells in Xander's ear, "Are all these bars for prostitution?"

"Not all of them," Xander yells back.

"How can you tell?" She yells back.

"Well, if they have sexy dress women yelling (sexy man) is a dead giveaway." He laughs and yells at Isabella, "If you're not interested going with them. They usually will be respectful of your wishes."

After 10 mins of walking, they make a right into the hotel's alley. As they near the hotel, a couple of girls run out of a bar and stop Isabella. "Come inside and have a drink, please," one of the girls asks Isabella. "Because of the rain, we have no customers," she expresses as she looks at Iseballa with a sad face.

"Xander, stop!" Isabella yells as she walks into the bar with the Thai girl. "Let's have one drink or coffee."

"What would you like to drink?" One of the bar staff asks.

"Do you have any coffee?" Isabelle answers her back. "Hey, what do you want to drink? She asks Xander. "I'm buying."

"We have to make some more coffee," the bartender explains to Isabella. "It will take 10 mins. We don't have any milk or creamer for the coffee," she says in her broken English.

"I like my coffee black," Isabelle tells the bartender as she takes a seat.

"Hey, I'm going to the 7-11 down the street to get some milk for my coffee and a top-up card for my phone," Xander says as he puts his poncho back on and then walks out into the rain.

Isabella is sitting, and a short time later, one of the girls working in the bar asks her if she could sit with her. "Sure," Isabella answers as she moves her chair over for her.

"I'm Yoyo." What's your name?" The Thai girl asks.

"My name is Isabella," she answers back. "Yoyo, I like your name."

"Thank you. It's short for Yotaka," she answers and takes a sip of her beer. "Where did your boyfriend go?" She asks.

"He is not my boyfriend," Isabella answers back. "Your English is very good. Have you lived in an English-speaking country before?" She asks.

"Thank you," Yoyo smiles back. "No, I taught myself English Grammar from school, reading books and watching English-speaking movies."

"I think you speak better English than my friend that just left," Isabella laughs and asks. "Are you from Pattaya?"

"No, I'm from a town called Udon Thani," Yoyo answers. "Not your boyfriend?" She asks as she gives Isabella a wink. "Is he gay?"

Isabella starts laughing. "No, he is not gay." "We were together but just friends now."

"I can see it in his eyes; he still cares for you," Yoyo says as she takes another drink.

"Yes, I still care for him too. It just didn't work," Izzy says.

"What happened?" Yoyo asks as she gives Isabella some water. "He is very handsome."

"I don't like to talk about it," Isabelle answers as she tries to hold a smile. "How did you end up working here?" As she tries to change the subject.

"Sorry to ask you," Yoyo moves in a little closer to Isabella. "Three years ago, my father got very sick. He couldn't work for many months, and we needed money for our farm. One of my friends told me about working at this bar. She asked if I could be the manager here because of my English," she explains as she stands up and points to a computer near the bar. "If you want to play some music, you can get on YouTube," she says as she walks back to the bar to talk to her staff.

Isabella walks over and scrolls on the computer for a few minutes, then clicks on YouTube, types in (Jeff Buckley-Hallelujah), and sits back down as the song plays.

Yoyo comes back to the table with Isabella's coffee and sits back down. "I know this song." "I heard it at my school as a girl," she utters as she slides her chair closer to Isabella. "I went to a Christian Thai school as a girl. My father wanted me to have a good education, so I didn't have to work on the farm," she says as she looks at Isabella, and a tear rolls down her face.

Isabella sees her tears and rubs Yoyo on the shoulder and tells her, "You don't have to tell me about this."

"It's OK," as Yoyo wipes the tears from her eyes. "My father died not too long ago. We were very close. He would take me everywhere with him." Yoyo grabs Isabella's hand on her shoulder. "He worked very hard to take care of my family, and he loved us very much."

"I'm sorry to hear about your dad," says Isabella as she takes a sip of her coffee.

"Thank you," says Yoyo as she starts to smile. "I don't know why I told you this. Its hard for me to talk to some of the other girls that work here. You had a very kind face. And sometimes, I get emotional," she said as she had her English to Thai App for the right word.

Isabella looks at her, smiles back, and answers, "I never really talked to a lot of people about what happened," as she sips her coffee. "You ask me what happened earlier. Xander, the guy that is with me. We were married at one time."

"Did he have another woman?" Yoyo asks.

"No, he didn't do anything like that," she answers back. "He was neglecting my feelings. And sometimes, he didn't even seem like he loved me." As she takes a big sigh. "And he never seems like he wanted children." She takes another sip of her coffee and pauses.

Yoyo shakes her head. "How long were you married?"

"We were together for 6 years and married for 1 year," she responds as she turns to look out the window. "I really loved him, but he treated me more like a friend than a wife," she says as she stands up to get a better look out the window. "I think he is coming back."

"I will get his coffee," says Yoyo as she gets up and walks over to the bar.

Xander walks in the front door, takes off his poncho, and proceeds over to Isabella. "Sorry it took so long," he says as he sits down. "It's still raining."

Yoyo returns to the table with Xander's coffee and sits down next to Isabella. "I'm Yoyo," she introduces herself as she greets him with a Wai (putting your hands together in small bow)

"I'm Xander," as he wai back.

"She has been keeping me company while you were gone," Isabella says, looks over at Xander and smiles. "I will be back in one moment." As she gets up to walk to the bathroom.

"Isabella is a very nice woman." Yoyo looks at Xander and smiles. "How is your coffee?"

"Isabella is my best friend. I would do anything for her," Xander says as he pours some of the milk into his coffee. "I've known her for a long time." Xander then adds 2 spoons of sugar to his coffee and takes a sip. "Coffee is good," He answers.

Yoyo smiles and asks. "What hotel are you staying in?"

"We are staying across the street at the Sabai Lodge," he answers while reaching into his back pocket.

"What do you have there?" Yoyo asks.

"I saw this while walking to 7-11 and thought Isabella would like it," he says as he shows her a necklace made from seashells. "It's nothing expensive, but It's very beautiful, like her."

"That's very sweet. I'm sure she will love it," Yoyo says, then walks away to the pool table and talks to a girl playing pool. Moments later, Yoyo returns and points to the girl at the pool table. "Would you like to play pool with her?" She asks.

"Sure," Xander answers and walks over and introduces himself, and grabs a que stick.

Isabella returns from the bathroom, sits down, looks over at Xander playing pool, and notices he is looking in her direction. He gives her a small wave and returns to the game.

Yoyo leans into Isabella and says, "He still loves you. I can see how he looks at you. I see a lot of men come in this bar and talk to my girls. Some speak, (bullshit) I think that is the right word you say in English, and some speak from their heart."

"He really broke my heart, and I didn't see him as the same man anymore," she explains as she finishes up her coffee. "He would be very nice one day, and the next, he would get upset over small things." She pauses and takes a deep breath. "He became unattractive to me."

"Sorry, what does unattractive mean?" Yoyo asks.

"It means ugly," answers Isabella

"Ugly?" Yoyo reacts, surprised. "He is a very handsome man!"

"No, not on the outside, but on the inside," Isabella answers back. "This has been going on for a couple of years, and last year he got worse." Isabella takes a sip of water. "He was on his phone too much and not paying attention to me. He hardly ever wanted to make love to me."

"You're a beautiful woman. Was there something wrong with him?" She says as she motions for one of her staff to get Isabella some more water.

"Do you know what Testosterone is?" She asks.

Yoyo grabs her phone and types in Testosterone on her English to Thai app. And then shakes her head. "Yes. I understand now."

"For the last 2 years, I've been trying to get him to go to the doctor to get it tested out," Isabella says as she turns to see Xander coming back to the table.

"You want to play a game with me?" Xander asks Isabella.

Isabella looks at Xander with a smile. "No, I'm OK at the moment." Then she watches Xander turn around and go back to the pool table.

"He said he would go to the Doctor but then make excuses. He finally went to see a doctor after I moved out," Isabella says as she takes a drink of her water. "Then we stayed in a halfway-built cabin with no electricity or water. I didn't even have a bathroom," she expressed, as a scowling look came on her face.

Yoyo nods her head and asks, "Why would you build a home like that in America?" she pauses. "I lived that way when I was a little girl before my dad got a better job. I remember it being tough."

"It was OK at first until it got hot," as she starts to describe the cabin. "I told him several times to get a bigger AC, but it's like he didn't care. I had goats and chickens, and it was out in nature. I really miss that part of my life out there, and sometimes I miss talking with him in the evening. He was really nice too. He brought me a car when my truck died. He would help me out with money sometimes. And we went on a lot of trips together. But the last few months we were there, he got worse."

Yoyo gets more comfortable in her chair and asks Isabella, "Why did you move out there with him?"

"We were married and thought he would love me more once we moved into the cabin," Isabella answers and looks over at Xander, still playing pool. "We did have some good times out there, too."

"Sorry, that happened to you. Nice to see you are still friends," Yoyo explains. "A lot of my girlfriends have relationship problems. It's because the guy drinks too much or doesn't work and makes his wife support him or has another woman."

"Xander only drank on special occasions, and he didn't cheat on me, and he worked very hard," Isabella responds. "I used to work for him, so I know he worked hard. He was often stressed out about work."

"Did you try to talk to him or give him? How do you say this word?" Yoyo hands Isabella her phone to show her the word.

"Ultimatum," answers Isabella, "No, I never gave him an ultimatum," Isabella sighs. "I did talk to him a few times about some of my concerns and problems. But he acted like it was no big deal, or he changed for a little while then went back to how he was."

"Men have heads like stone. Hard for them to understand sometimes," Yoyo tells her. "What if he changed and loved you the way you deserved."

"I don't think it would be real, and he probably would just go back to how he was," Isabella explains in disappointment and then says, "He has been really nice on this trip and seems to be going out of his way to make me happy."

"I have seen a lot of men with broken hearts totally change their whole life for love," Yoyo tells her as she starts to smile at Isabella. "Not easy to find a good man. And sometimes the good man just needs the right motivation."

"I don't want to talk about this anymore. It makes me a little sad," Isabella says, and she watches Xander return to the table.

"You ready to go back to the hotel?" Xander asks.

"No, I'm going to stay here a little longer and talk with Yoyo, but you go ahead," she says, then asks, "What time are you planning on getting up?"

"How about 9 am? We can meet in the lobby," Xander answers and then reaches into his pocket. "I almost forgot to give this to you," As he hands Isabella the seashell necklace. "I thought it would look very beautiful on you."

"Awe! Thank you. That was very kind of you," Isabella says with a big smile.

"Nice to meet you, Yoyo and please take very good care of Isabella," Xander says and puts on his poncho and walks out the door.

"See, I told you; he still loves you," Yoyo says as she helps fasten the necklace on Isabella. "Soy Mak," she says in Thai, which means very beautiful.

"Kap Kun Ka (Thank you)," Isabella answers back in Thai.

"Do you want any more coffee?" Yoyo asks.

"No, I don't want any more coffee. I will just finish the rest of the milk Xander left here," she answers as she takes the cap of the bottle.

Isabella remained at the bar for another hour, talking with Yoyo. They add each other to Facebook and start looking at each other's pictures. Afterward, they promise to keep in contact. As Isabella is about to leave, she stops and asks Yoyo, "Can I pray over you?"

Yoyo grabs Isabella's hand and utters, "Yes. I have not had anyone pray over me since I went to school."

Isabella leads them in prayer as they hold each other's hand. After the prayer, they embrace each other. The rain is still falling, so Isabella puts her poncho on while Yoyo grabs an umbrella. Both walk to the hotel across the street. One final hug as they say their goodbyes.

Chapter 6: Hippie Haven

Isabella steps out of the elevator and walks over to Xander, who is sitting down in the lobby.

"Sorry, I'm a few minutes late." She says as she sits down across from Xander. "How did you sleep?" She asks.

"I slept OK. How about yourself?" He answers and then asks.

Isabella answers, "I think I had the best night's sleep since I've been in Thailand." and asks. "What time are we heading back to Bangkok?"

"Not in a rush, but we have to check out at noon," Xander replies as he grabs his coffee. "You want anything?"

"No, thank you," Isabella says as she opens up her purse. "Would you mind if I get a coffee with Yoyo?" She asked me if I had time to call her and if we could have a coffee down the street at a café."

"Yeah, I guess so," Xander says as a look of disappointment comes across his face. "Be back here at 12:00 pm, please."

"Can I use your phone, please?" Isabella asks as she grabs Yoyo's number from her purse. "I'm going to call her."

Xander hands her the phone and continues to drink his coffee. After the phone call. Isabella tells Xander, "You can go ahead and get breakfast. Yoyo will be here in 20mins." As she hands the phone back and explains. "You don't need to wait for me."

"I will stick around here until Yoyo arrives. I like to find out where you guys are going," Xander comments.

Yoyo arrives at 9:38 am, and they all have a brief conversation. Yoyo tells Xander that they are going to the beach, just a short walk from the hotel to a café that a friend owns. They tell Xander,

"Goodbye," as they turn around and walk away. Xander's face crumples as he slowly walks backward and watches them until they are out of his view.

"He looked a little sad," Yoyo remarks as they are walking down the ally.

"Yes, I noticed that. He needs to get used to doing more things by himself," Isabella answered back and then expressed, "We need to be back in 2 hours. I promised him I would be back."

"Not a problem," Yoyo answers. "Thanks for joining me this morning."

Yoyo and Isabella continue walking to the end of the alley as they cross the road. Yoyo points to a small hut with a few tables behind some palm trees. "This is my friend's little café," Yoyo tells Isabella.

"Cute place; thank you for taking me," Isabella comments, then takes a seat.

Yoyo asks, "Black Coffee, right?" as she walks up to the counter.

"Yes, please," she answers back while looking at the sea crashing onto the beach.

Yoyo returns with their coffees and takes a seat next to Isabella. "After you left last night. I was looking at more of your pictures on Facebook," Yoyo comments. "Your wedding pictures were Amazing!" She then gets out her phone to ask questions about Isabella's Facebook page.

"Thank you," Isabella answers back, then takes a sip of coffee.

"I saw a lot of animals in your pictures. Goats, chickens, and different dogs." Yoyo comments, then shows Isabella a picture and asks. "Where is this picture? You look very happy," she says as she gives the phone to Isabella.

"That was on my honeymoon, the very first day we got there," Isabella answers. "The animals were from our little farm."

"Xander looks a little fat here," Yoyo says as she laughs

"Which picture are you talking about?" Asks Isabella.

"This one here of you kissing him on the cheek," Yoyo replies and shows Isabella the Facebook photo.

Isabella leans over and comments, "That one was on our honeymoon, too." Then laughs, "Yeah, he does look fat in that photo."

"Well, he doesn't look fat now," Yoyo answers back.

Yoyo continues to scroll through Isabella's pictures and occasionally makes comments. "You were a Nok Muay?" Thai for Thai boxer.

"Yes, I trained very hard for about three years and had four fights," Isabella answers and looks at Yoyo with a grin. "Actually, that's where I met Xander. He was my coach."

"Wow!" Yoyo says in excitement as she looks at Isabella and continues to scroll through pictures. "You and Xander did a lot of things together. Looks like a lot of great memories," she says and pauses. "Sorry, it didn't work. You guys looked like a happy couple."

"One last question," Yoyo asks. "You had black hair before? I saw one picture of you and Xander, and he has a Trump Hat on."

Isabella laughs and answers. "Yes, that was me. That picture was of our very first trip together." Isabella takes a small sip of her coffee. "I couldn't look at any of your pictures other than the few you showed me last night. My phone doesn't work unless I have Wifi," she informs Yoyo.

Yoyo smiles and comments, "Let me go to my page."

Next 30mins Yoyo shows Isabella pictures on Facebook of places she has been, her family, and life in Pattaya. And then says, "Well, let me put my phone away, and we can enjoy this beautiful morning." As they continue to talk about life.

After 2 hrs. of talking in the café. Isabella stands up and tells Yoyo. "I need to go back to the hotel. I have to meet Xander at noon."

"I will walk with you," Yoyo answers as she stands up.

They arrive back at the hotel at 11:47 am and see Xander waiting down in the lobby. He looks over and sees Isabella and Yoyo and motions for Isabella. "Hey, you need to go get your bag. We must check out in 10 minutes." Xander frantically expresses.

"OK, Ok, Ok," Isabella answers as she turns to Yoyo and says. "Well, thank you for taking me to get coffee." She gives her a hug. "I will keep in contact with you through Facebook." She says as she turns to walk to the elevator.

Yoyo walks over to Xander and tells him, "Hey, you make sure you take very good care of her and always listen to her." She then Wai Xander and said in Thai, "sa-wat-dii ka," then exited the hotel.

Xander walks over to the counter and begins to check out. Isabella returns to the lobby to check out with Xander. She turns to him and says, "Thank you so much for taking me here yesterday. I had a really good time." As she looks at him, she smiles and asks, "What's our plan now?"

"We need to get a taxi and head back to Bangkok," Xander answers as he turns and walks to the front door into the alley.

There are several taxi parks out front. Xander walks up to the first Taxi and asks the driver, "Bangkok?"

The driver shakes his head no.

Xander walks to another taxi and asks. "Bangkok?"

"5000 Baht," The second driver says.

"No, thank you, that's too much," Xander says as he picks up two of the bags and looks over at a taxi dropping someone off. "We need to go to Bangkok?" He yells as the driver rolls down the window and looks at Xander.

The Taxi driver smiles and nods his head. "2500 Baht?" He says as he pops the trunk. "Where in Bangkok?"

"Soy Khaosan," Xander answers as he grabs their bags and places them in the trunk.

After they both enter the taxi, Isabella asks, "Where are we going now in Bangkok?"

"We are going to Khaosan Road," Xander answers as he looks at Isabella with a smile.

"Yay! That's one of the places I want to see in Bangkok," she says, then reaches into her bag to pull out the Lonely Planet Book.

"Try to stay awake this time," he says as she pauses. "You can see the countryside of Thailand," Xander explains.

"I will try my best. But you know how I am in cars," she says, then she laughs.

3:51 Lamphuhouse Bangkok 1 Block from Khaosan Road.

Isabella steps out of the taxi and looks around at the shophouses and narrow streets, with all the tourists walking around and the smell of chili peppers burning her nose. "Is this Khaosan Road?" She asks. "I thought it would be a little bigger than this," she says as she grabs her bag out of the trunk.

"No. Khasan Road is one block away," Xander comments as he grabs the other two bags. "This area is like 6 or 8 square blocks with all kinds of shop houses, bars, restaurants, massage shops, and hotels." He continues, "The Kings Palace is walking distance from here." As he points to his left, "And there are a couple of old temples around here, too."

"I like the vibe around here," she says as they start walking into the courtyard.

"This place is more popular with the younger crowds and backpackers," Xander says as he follows behind.

"I noticed," she comments as they walk up to the front desk to check-in.

"Do you remember watching the movie (The Island) with your husband in it?" (referring to Leonardo DiCaprio) Xander asks as he starts to chuckle.

"Yes, I remember that movie," she answers as she starts to laugh.

Xander grabs the room key and says, "Parts of the movie were filmed around here somewhere."

Isabella shakes her head and then comments, "This boutique hotel is very cute." Isabella expresses, "It's very retro."

As they start walking up the stairs, Xander mentions, "Our room is on the 3rd floor, and they don't have an elevator."

"Good exercise, but you're going back down to grab the big bag," she says as she laughs.

Xander laughs as well.

Twenty steps later and a short walk down the hallway. They reach their room on the 3rd floor. As they enter the room, Xander puts the bag down and tells Isabella, "I'm going back to the front desk to get our other bag; go ahead and pick which bed you want."

"How long are we staying at this hotel?" She asks.

"We are only in Bangkok for three more days. I was thinking we just stay here the remainder of the time unless you want to change," he says as he exits the room.

As Xander returns to the room, he can hear Isabella singing in the shower and notices she has already claimed the bed next to the balcony. He walks over to the balcony and looks down onto the street as he hears Isabella ask from the shower, "What are our plans this evening?"

"There are so many restaurants and shops around here. You would spend days walking around looking at everything." Xander answered back.

Isabella steps out of the bathroom. "So, we are just going to wing it?" Isabella asks as she grabs a small bag and heads back into the bathroom.

"Yes." - "The best way to describe this area is it's like Bourbon Street, Bonnaroo, and Woodstock all rolled up into one area." Xander hollers at Isabella in the bathroom.

"OK, sounds great. Give me about 15mins, please." Isabella yells back from the bathroom.

4:47 pm Khaosan Road

Xander and Isabella turn right out of the side alley and walk a few steps onto Khaosan Road. Isabella's eyes light up as she sees all the street vendors on either side of the street, the chatter and laughter of people, and the cafes, hotels, and bars that line up either side of the road.

"I can see why you got a hotel a block away. It is very noisy here." Isabella says as she starts to walk down the street. "How long is this street?" She asks.

"It's around ¼ mile long, but you have another street over there, but not as busy. And the side streets where our hotel is at." Xander answers back and asks, "You want to try a banana pancake?" They walk by a street food cart with a griddle.

"Yes, that sounds great, waffle daddy!" (a nickname she called Xander when they were together) Isabella comments back and smiles.

Xander laughs, and he orders one pancake.

They both watch as the vendor pulls out a little ball of Roti dough and throws it down on a tray. Splat! As he starts kneading the dough flat. He then picks it up like pizza dough, spins it around in the air, and throws it down on the griddle. The sound of dough sizzling in the butter and the aroma of the pancake fill the air. The vendor then grabs a banana and starts dicing paper thin slices onto the pancake. He then gets a spatula, folds the pancake in half, and asks us. "You want chocolate and sugar?" As he flips the pancake over.

"Yes, both," Isabella answers as she watches him slide the pancake on a paper plate. "Cut it into small squares. Then sprinkle some brown sugar and a few thin lines of chocolate on the top." He then inserts two toothpicks and hands it to Xander.

"Wow, that looks so good!" Isabella says in anticipation as Xander grabs a square and puts it into her mouth. "That is delicious!" She exclaims.

They both continue to walk down the street and periodically stop to look at clothing, homemade jewelry, and local art. Suddenly, the sound of hip-hop drowns out the street noise, and a large crowd of people gather around to watch some street performers breakdance.

"They are very good," Xander says to Isabella as he drops a 100 baht note inside their bucket.

"This is like a Thai verse of Bourbon Street!" Isabella shouts at Xander as they carry on walking further.

"Yes, that's the best way to describe this area from an American perspective," Xander responds back and jokingly says, "But now you can drink."

Isabella turns around, looks at Xander, and asks, "Are you referring to our trip to New Orleans?"

"Yes. I remember you wanted to go to Bourbon Street for Halloween, but since you were only twenty. You couldn't go into any of the bars." Xander explains, "That was one of my favorite trips with you."

Isabella responds, "I would have been happy just to walk down the street that evening."

"Yes, I know, but we didn't bring the right clothes with us," Xander says. "Remember it was going to get cold that evening," as Xander points to a guy hiding off the side between two vendors with a cardboard box on the ground and a couple of boxes of Viagra on top.

Isabella starts to laugh and asks. "Are they allowed to sell that on the street like that?"

"I don't think so, and it might be fake," he says as he chuckles back, "We can find out this evening if it is real," as he looks at Isabella and smiles.

"Ha-ha, not funny," Isabella says sarcastically back.

As they keep strolling, they come to the end of Khaosan Road. Xander gets his phone out of his pocket to check the time. "It's almost 6:30. Do you want to get something to eat?" Xander asks.

"Yes," she answers and asks, "You want to go to one of the Israeli restaurants we saw earlier?"

"Sounds good to me," he answers as they both turn around to start walking back in the other direction.

6:47 pm Jerusalem Café

Xander and Isabella walk up to the hostess. "Shalom," the hostess says in Hebrew. "Just you two?" She asks as she points to a table. They take a seat and start looking through the menu.

"Anything looking good?" Xander asks.

"I'm thinking about the vegetarian platter with humus," Isabella says as she points at the menu. "How about yourself?"

"I think I will get the same thing," Xander answers.

"What do you want to do after we have dinner?" Isabella asks as she looks around in the restaurant.

"Good question; I'm sure we could go dancing or karaoke," Xander answers. "I think some of the places will start opening soon." Xander pauses, then utters, "We can just walk around and see what's open or go barhopping too. We will figure it out."

"I trust you since you're the expert. I just don't want to drink," Isabella explains. "Are you ready to order?" She asks Xander as the waitress walks up to the table.

8:09 pm Khaosan Road outside of Jerusalem Café.

"Which direction do you want to go?" Xander asks as he looks at Isabella.

Isabella leans into Xander's ear and says, "It's much louder out here now, like walking through downtown Nashville with all the music coming from all the bars."

Xander nods his head and yells, "Let's walk back over there," as he points in the direction where they first started on Khaosan Road.

Isabella grabs Xander's bicep as he leads her through the crowds of people on the street. As they are walking, they pass a Reggae pub. "That would be a nice place to go," Xander says in Isabella's ear as they continue walking. Then, they pass a bar that caters to more of the Thai Crowd. As they move along, they see a club with hip-hop and another with techno. "We are almost to the end of the road," Xander comments.

"How about we go to Reggae Pub?" Isabella asks as she pulls Xander's arm to stop. She then notices a street vendor selling a few items inspired by mushrooms. "Let's stop here for a sec. I can maybe find my dad a gift," she explains.

Isabella looks through their t-shirts and a few necklaces and asks Xander, "What do you think?"

"Well, I don't see him wearing a necklace," Xander answers as he points to some salt and pepper shakers in the shape of mushrooms. "I think he would like this," he comments.

Isabella buys two T-shirts for her dad and the salt and pepper shaker Xander pointed to. Then, she leans and asks, "Are you ready to walk to Reggae pub?" She then grabs Xander's bicep again.

Xander nods his head yes and grabs the bag as they start walking.

9:21 pm Reggae Pub

As they take a seat inside the pub, Isabella leans in and asks. "Can you order me a water? Isabella stands back up, starts moving her hips, and says, "I can't do that Reggae dance thing you do." She then laughs and starts twerking for a few seconds.

Xander laughs as he starts to order a beer and water from the waitress for her. Xander moves a little closer, puts his hands on Isabella's hips, and starts to move along with her in steps with the music. Isabella turns around, puts her hand gently on his chest while still dancing, and pushes herself away. Then yells, "Dance with one of the girls here."

"I'm OK," Xander says as he steps off to her side and asks, "Why do you keep trying to get me to dance with someone else?"

"Because we are not together, and I want you to move on," she answers and states, "You can find some girl here."

"That is not me anymore," Xander answers back as he moves in a little closer to talk. "My life changed when I met you," he comments as he looks at her with a smile.

She smiles back and says, "You're my friend, and I want you to meet a nice girl someday," as she starts dancing again.

Xander looks away as his smile leaves his face. He takes a seat and starts drinking his beer.

A few moments later, Isabella sits back down and asks. "You, OK?"

"I'm fine," Xander answers with a grin on his face and expresses, "You know you were my best friend, but you don't even want me around." As he stands up, "It's hard because the last 6 years we were together every day." As he takes a sip of his beer, he continues, "There were only a few occasions we were only apart for a few days."

"You don't think it's hard for me?" Isabella quickly answers.

"Well, honestly, I don't know," Xander answers, then mumbles, "Definitely not as hard as me. You had your parents you ran to; I was left with an empty house and your animals to take care of."

"What did you say?" Isabella asks.

"Nothing. I'm sorry I brought this up," Xander expresses as he moves away from Isabella. "I'm going to the bathroom," he says as he tries to hide a tear in his eye.

Xander walks into the bathroom, splashes water on his face, and says to himself, "Keep it together, Xander; remember the past is past; she doesn't want to hear that, and talking about that will make her wall taller, smile and be happy that she came with you to Thailand." He looks at himself in the mirror, smiles, and returns to the table.

As Xander is sitting down, Isabella leans over and says, "You missed it. While you were gone, two guys almost got into a fight."

"Darn," he says as he looks at Isabella with a smile. "I apologize for the early."

"That's OK," she says as she hooks her arm around his, then puts her head on his shoulder. "You were my best friend, too," she lets go and says, "I need to go to the restroom now."

DJ starts playing Bob Marley (Could You Be Loved) as Isabella returns, grabs Xander's hand, and pulls him on the dance floor. As they start dancing, Xander looks into her eyes and comments, "I haven't heard this song since we were on our Honeymoon."

Isabella smiles and leans into his ear, "You mean when we were riding around next to the beach."

Xander nods yes and smiles back. He leans back and whispers in her ear, "Do you still remember our wedding song dance?" As he grabs her hands.

Isabella whispers back, "I don't think we should do that." She slightly pushes him away.

"Sorry," Xander says as he steps back and continues to dance.

After a few more songs, Isabella asks, "Hey, you want to go somewhere else?"

"Sure, we can walk out and decide." Answers Xander.

11:09 pm Khaosan Road outside the entrance of the Reggae Pub

"It was hard to talk in there," Isabella explains, and she starts looking around at the surroundings.

"What are you looking for?" Xander asks.

Isabella keeps looking left and right and then answers, "I want to get another banana pancake; it was good."

Xander points to the right and says, "The one we were at earlier is that way."

After getting a banana pancake, Isabella tells Xander, "Let's go to the Cigar Bar we saw earlier."

11:41 pm Hemingways Cigar Bar

Xander and Isabella are greeted by a cloud of smoke as they enter the door. The smell of leather, teak wood furniture, and the sweet aroma of cigars fill the air. Isabella walks up to the bar and looks through the glass case to choose which cigar to smoke. Xander tells Isabella, "I am going to grab the table we passed by as we walked in."

"OK, I will get you a beer," Isabella answers back.

Isabella returns to the table and sits back down. Hands Xander his beer. Grabs the cigar and puts it into her mouth, strikes a match, brings the flame to the cigar, and takes a puff. She leans her head back and blows the smoke in the air. "Do you like the beer?" She asks.

"How did you know I liked Beer Lao Dark?" Xander answers back.

Isabella smiles and comments, "I know you like dark beers, and that's the only dark beer they sell."

Xander laughs, then takes a sip and notices Isabella looking off in the distance. "You want to be quiet, don't you? He asks.

Isabella nods yes and says, "I'm just enjoying my cigar."

Xander pulls his phone out, responds to some messages, and lets Isabella be with her thoughts. Around 15 minutes later, Xander asks, "You, OK?"

"Yes, I'm fine. I just want to be quiet," she answers, takes a few more puffs, and says. "Are you ready to head back to the hotel?"

"That's fine with me if its OK with you?" He answers back.

12:22 am Khaosan Road

Not much was said as they exited the bar and walked down Khaosan Road. Some of it was the noise volume, and the other was Isabella being deep in thought.

As they are about to enter the courtyard of the hotel at 12:46 am, Isabella turns around and asks Xander, "Have you tried any dating apps lately?"

Xander answers, "I did for about two or three days after you sent me a rude text message about three months ago. Then, I deleted the account. I thought this was stupid."

"Why is it stupid? Maybe you can meet someone," she says as they start walking up the steps.

Xander didn't respond and continued to follow Issabella up the steps.

"Hello, did you hear me?" Isabella asks.

"Yes, I heard you," he answers as they make it to the next level.

"Why don't you answer?" Isabella unpleasantly asks.

As they reach the 3rd floor, Xander answers back, "I really don't want to talk about that," as he tries to hide the disappointed look on his face. "I'm going to take a quick shower; that way, you can have the bathroom to yourself."

Xander opens the door and goes into the bathroom to shower. Isabella grabs her phone and connects it to the Wi-Fi. 5 min later, Xander comes out of the bathroom and says, "It's all yours."

Isabella takes a relaxing shower for 10 minutes. As she lets the hot water pound on her back while thinking, she starts to mumble to herself, "Xander, why do you make this so hard?"

Isabella exits out of the bathroom with a towel wrapped around her. She notices Xander still awake and says to him, "I'm going to sit out on the balcony and smoke another one of these cigars,"

"You have a good night," Xander says as he turns over.

"Hey," Isabella says as Xander turns back over.

"I had a good time tonight," she says as she starts to slide the balcony door open. "You have a good night."

Chapter 7: The Fight

The sound of tuk-tuk (3-wheeler taxi) passing by on the street and the sunlight shining through the balcony wakes up Xander. He grabs his phone to look at the time. 6:47 am. Xander sits up in bed and looks over at Isabella. Her feet are by the headboard, and her head is under some pillows at the foot of the bed. He yawns, gets out of bed, and walks over to her bed. "Hey, hey," he says as he tries to untangle the comforter wrapped around Isabella.

"Mmmmm, what time is it?" She asks.

"It's like almost 7," Xander answers as he starts walking to the bathroom.

"Can you get me up at 7:30 am, please?" She asks, as her muffled voice comes from out under the pillows.

Xander goes into the bathroom to take a shower and get ready to start the day.

"Hey, Izzy!" Xander says as he removes the pillow from her head. "It's 7:30."

"OK, Ok," she answers as she pushes herself up and kneels on the bed. A look of confusion comes on her face as she notices herself at the foot of the bed. "Can you get me some water and coffee, please?" She asks as she rises out of bed.

Xander looks over at Isabella and breaks out into laughter.

"What is so funny?" she exclaims. Just then, she looked into the mirror on the wall and noticed her mascara smeared down her right cheek, looking like a raccoon. "Oh shit! I forgot to wash the makeup off last night," she expresses as she tries to push down her hair, which looks like some rockstar from the 1980s. She looks at Xander and smiles, then gives him the middle finger.

Xander is still laughing. "I'm going to go downstairs and get you water and coffee," he says as he opens the door.

Isabella smiles back and says, "I'm going to get ready," as she turns away from the mirror and walks toward the bathroom.

9:05 The hotel's restaurant

"What's our plan today?" Isabella asks as she starts to take a bite of the fruit salad she ordered for breakfast.

"I was thinking we could walk to the King's Palace and do a tour there," Xander answers as he spreads butter on his toast.

"You're just winging it, aren't you?" She asks.

Xander takes a bite of his toast and puts his index finger in the air, signaling one second while he is chewing. "What do you mean?" He asks.

"You know how I like to plan things out in advance," she answers as she takes a sip of her coffee.

"Well, Khaosan Road changes all the time, so I don't know what is there," Xander answers back. "Besides, if I told you where we are going, would it make a difference?" He asks as he takes a bite of his bacon. "I thought I did a good job in Pattaya!" He exclaims in a louder voice.

"Don't have to get defensive!" Isabella responds back as she finishes the last of the fruit salad.

"I'm not getting defensive," Xander explains.

Isabella finishes her coffee and tells him, "You started raising your voice."

"Well, sorry. I just thought I was being an awesome tour guide," Xander says back in his normal speaking voice. "You ready to get out of here?" He asks as he motions for the check.

"You have been a great tour guide," she answers, looking and smiling at him.

As they walk out of the hotel restaurant and step into the alley, Xander asks Isabella, "You want to take a tuk-tuk to the King's Palace?"

"Yes, sure," she says in excitement. "I've been wanting to ride in one of these since we got here. How come we haven't yet?" She asks.

Xander waves at a tuk-tuk driver down the road, turns to Isabella, and answers. "Why haven't we taken one of these? It is because you must haggle with them, and they always overcharge foreigners."

The tuk-tuk pulls up, and Xander asks the driver, "Kings Palace."

"200 baht," The driver says.

"No Thanks," he says as he starts walking away.

The driver puts the tuk-tuk in reverse and meets up with Xander, who is walking back to Isabella. "100 baht," he says.

"75 baht," Xander haggles back with him.

The driver hesitates for a moment and says, "OK," as Xander turns to Isabella to help her climb into the back seat.

The driver puts the tuk-tuk in gear and starts to speed away. Isabella's hair blows around in the open air as she shouts in Xander's ear. "This thing is very noisy," she exclaims as she tries to hold her hair in place.

"Yeah, that's another reason I prefer a taxi, but they can be pretty exciting, too," Xander yells back.

"How much would it have been if we took a taxi?" Isabella asks.

"It would most likely be 50 baht if there is no traffic. 20- or 30-minute walk. I think," Xander answers as he starts to point over to his left.

Isabella looks to her left across a huge grass field at a 20ft tall stone wall that's wrapped around a two or three city block compound. "Is that the Kings' Palace behind that wall?" Isabella asks.

"Yes, that's it," Xander answers.

"Looks like a castle wall, like something you see in England," she says in excitement as she looks back at Xander.

"Yes, it kind of does," he says as he looks back at Isabella. "You know I've never been here before."

The Tuk-tuk arrives at the tourist entrance of King Palace. Xander and Isabella queue in line to enter. As they get closer to the entrance, they notice a sign saying, "No shorts allowed," and another sign that says, "Tours closed for Royal Residents- outside grounds open."

Isabella looks at Xander and says, "We both have shorts on," as she notices a street vendor across the street that is selling Sarongs.

"Stay here in line, and I will go get us two," Xander says as he jumps out of line to the vendor.

Xander returns and hands one of the Sarongs to Isabella. "They charge 300 baht for one of these," Xander says in an exasperated tone.

"Is that expensive?" She asks as she starts to wrap the Sarong around her waist.

"Yes, the vendors at Khaosan Road charge around 100," Xander answers as he tries to figure out how to put the Sarong on.

"300 baht, that's around $10.00 US?" Isabella asks as she steps closer to the entrance.

"Yes, something like that," Xander says as he gets his phone out to show the tickets to staff at the entrance.

10:23 inside the front entrance of Kings Palace.

Isabella and Xander marvel at the luxurious Palace with its bright white stone walls, its red tile roof trimmed in gold, and its three golden Pagodas. As they tour the grounds, they are mesmerized by all the gold leaf and neatly trimmed hedges and bushes that adorn the Palace Grounds.

"This place might outdo the Biltmore Mansion," Isabella says, as her eyes are as bright as diamonds.

Xander shakes his head in agreement and says, "Can you imagine living here? Too bad we couldn't go inside the Royal Residents."

"Does the Royal Family still live here?" Isabella asks.

"No, I think this is mostly used for ceremonial activities, probably why the inside is closed," Xander explains.

Isabella and Xander wander around for another two and a half hrs on an unguided tour as they periodically stop to take some pictures or read some information.

As they both exit the King's Palace and start removing their Sarongs, Xander asks Isabella, "Do you want to walk or take a taxi back to the Khaosan Road area?

"You said it's about a 30-minute walk, correct?" Isabella answers as she points to street vendors selling water. "I need water; do you want one as well?"

"Yeah, I will take a water," Xander answers as he shakes his head yes.

"I'm OK to walk," she says as she hands the water to Xander.

Isabella looks over at Xander and notices him not talking a lot. "You, OK? You haven't talked much today?

"Yeah, I'm fine. I just got something on my mind," He answers.

2:49 Hotel

Isabella and Xander enter the courtyard of the hotel. Xander stops and says, "Hey, go ahead and get ready for this evening and wear something very nice," as he starts walking to the café. "I'm going to get a coffee while you get ready."

Isabella looks at Xander with a smile and says, "OK," she then turns to walk up the steps.

Around 40 minutes pass as Isabella opens the room door. She takes a step to the handrail and looks over onto the courtyard to see if she can see Xander. As she looks down, she can see Xander sitting at a table in the cafe, writing again. "Hey, Xander!" She yells from the 3rd floor.

Xander hears his name and looks around to see where Isabella is at.

"Hey, look up toward our room," Isabella yells again as she starts walking toward the stairs.

Xander's eyes light up as he looks at her as she steps off the stairs. She walks toward his table, spins around, and asks, "What do you think?"

"I'm speechless!" Xander blurts out as he looks her up and down in a flowery dress with a flower tucked in the side of her ear.

Isabella smiles and says, "I bought this dress about a month ago just for this trip."

"The colors of this dress and patterns are beautiful!" Xander explains as his grin gets bigger. "And I love your hair." Xander stands up and says, "I'm debating if this might have topped your look at the wedding."

"You really mean that?" Isabella says as she looks back at him.

"Yes, of course. - I'm going to get ready," he answers as he starts to head toward the stairs.

"OK, I will wait here. Oh, can you grab my black purse when you get to the room?" Isabella asks.

Xander returns to the café at 4:03 pm and sees Isabella sitting at the same table he was sitting at earlier. She looks up, reaches out to grab her purse, and says, "You look handsome."

"Thank you," he answers as he reaches out his hand to help her up. "The place we are going to is called (Sala Rattanakosin Eatery and Bar) next to the river," he continues as he pulls her up.

4:37pm Sala Rattanakosin Eatery and Bar

Xander and Isabella step out of the taxi and walk through the front door. Xander walks up to the hostess and asks for a table for two. He turns around to Isabella and says. "It will be a few minutes. We can go to the bar over there," as Xander points over his shoulder, "or we can go to the rooftop bar."

"I guess the rooftop bar," Isabella says.

Xander smiles and says, "Going to be a surprise in a few seconds," as he turns to walk to the rear of the restaurant.

Isabella follows behind. "What do you mean surprised?" she says, then takes a few more steps and looks across the river from the solid glass wall at the rear of the restaurant. "What temple is that?" She asks.

"It is called Wat Aru or Temple of the Dawn," Xander answers back as he turns to walk upstairs. "We can get a better view from the 2nd floor."

Isabella follows behind and remarks, "This is a wonderful surprise," as she reaches the top of the stairs.

"I think this is one of the oldest Temples in Bangkok. Built like in 1500 or something," Xander explains as he looks for two seats at the bar.

"I remember reading about this temple from the tour book I brought with me," she explains.

"Do you remember when it was built?" Xander asks as he helps Isabella in her seat.

Isabella sits down and turns her chair around where she can get a better look at the Temple, then answers, "I don't remember; I have to look it up again."

"Ankor Wat Temple in Cambodia looks similar to this," he says as he looks at the drink menu. "Except at Angkor Wat, the complex is bigger, and a lot more stone Temples everywhere."

"Too bad we couldn't stay longer and go to Cambodia," Isabella says.

"Yeah, too bad," Xander agrees, then asks. "You want to get a bottle of wine?"

Isabella stands up and answers, "No, I don't feel like drinking." She walks over to the balcony to take pictures on her phone.

Xander taps Izzy on her shoulder. "Our hostess is here; our table is ready," he says as he points at the hostess.

They follow the hostess downstairs to their table. Xander pulls the chair out for Isabella and then takes a seat. "What do you think of this place?" Xander asks.

"I say this is the nicest restaurant we have been to since we have been here," Izzy answers as she starts to look through the menu. "What makes this restaurant stand out is the view of Temple of Dawn."

"Yes, that's why I came here," Xander explains. "I have been here like three or four times," he says as he points to the dock at the river. "You see the dock right there?"

"Yes, what about it?" Isabella asks.

"Remember when we stayed at Shangri La hotel, and we saw the ferry boats and the water taxis?" Xander asks as he picks up the menu.

"Yes, I remember." She answers as she picks up her menu again.

"This is one of their drop-offs," Xander comments.

Isabella shakes her head, takes a sip of water, and comments, "It's mostly Thai food with a few Western choices."

"Have you decided what you want?" Xander asks.

"Yes, I think I will have the Sea Bass," Isabella says as she notices their waitress coming to the table.

"Hello, I'm Toon," the waitress says as she gets ready to take their order.

Isabella starts off, "I like to have the Grilled Sea Bass and the Morning Glory."

"I like to have the beef salad but just a little spicy and sticky rice," Xander says to the waitress.

"On a scale of 1 to 5, 5 being the hottest?" Toon asks Xander.

"Let's try 2," Xander says to Toon.

"You're going to like the Morning Glory," Xander says to Isabella. "It is some sort of vine."

5:21 Dinner has arrived.

Isabella looks down at her Sea Bass. "It's a whole fish," she exclaims.

Xander laughs and says, "You get a spoon or fork, push it into the side of the scales, and the skin should peel right off."

"It still has its head with spices and herbs stuffed down its mouth," Isabella says with curiosity.

Isabella grabs her fork and firmly pushes it onto the fish's tail. She gets a spoon and slides it against the fish scales, making it crack open. Next, she gets the fork under the skin, gently pulling it away and exposing the meaty white flesh. She digs the fork into the side of the fish, stabbing a hunk of fish onto her fork, and brings it to her lips. "Mmmm, this is some of the best tasting fish I have had," she says, then she fans her mouth. "It's Fucking Hot! Excuse my French."

"You alright?" Xander asks as he chuckles. "Take a drink of your water."

"How's your food?" Isabella asks as sweat forms on her forehead.

"Yes, it's very good, just a tad spicy," Xander answers.

"After dinner, we will go back upstairs to watch the sunset behind the temple," Xander explains. "The sun actually sets in between those Pagodas," as he points towards the Temple.

Toon approaches the table and asks, "Would you like any dessert or anything else?"

"Can we have our desert upstairs so we can watch the sunset?" Xander asks.

"Not a problem," Toon answers. "I will find you a seat near the balcony."

Xander and Isabella sit down near the balcony, and they can see the sun going into position above them. "What time does the sun set?" Isabella asks.

"I think it sets around 6:30, which is in 25 minutes," Xander says as he looks at his phone.

Isabella positions her chair around, facing away from the temple because the sun's rays are still very bright. "I will spin my chair back around when the sun gets closer," she explains as she sees Xander pull out some folded paper. "What do you have there?" She asks.

"Isabella, you know you were more than just my lover but also my best friend," Xander expresses as he unfolds the paper that was in his back pocket.

"Yes, you were my best friend too," Isabella answers as she looks down at the notes. "We both made an agreement that neither of us would get into a conversation about the past," she exclaims as she looks him in the eye.

"Please give me a few minutes, please," he says in an anxious tone.

Isabella starts to grin, leans back in her chair, and crosses her arms.

"I have been wanting to say so many things, so I wrote a lot of things down. Every time I try to talk to you, I would get emotional and say things I didn't mean to say, or it would come out wrong." He takes a deep breath. "I have written and re-written this so many times," he explains as he flips through some of the papers and then starts to read, "I took this breakup very hard. I guess now you can see I loved you very much. And for the first three months, I was very confused about what happened. I tried to get answers from your parents and friends. Was there something I didn't know about or something she mentioned to them about our relationship, I would ask," he pauses as he sees Isabella motion for the waitress.

"Toon, can I get a glass of wine, please," Isabella says, then looks back at Xander, "OK, continue," in a snappy tone.

"My head filled with so many thoughts. No close friends or family nearby that I could go visit. Besides you, I think your parents were my closest friends around here. I felt I lost who I was. I was alone."

Xander pauses, gets a drink of water, and then continues, "I felt so abandoned, but as I started to learn about myself, I was the one who abandoned you. When you told me about some of the issues you had with me, I often would tell you I would get to it after the work season was over or that issue would solve itself. At that moment! I should have stopped what I was doing, looked you in the eyes, and asked you how we could solve this problem together. I made the mistake that the majority of men make. We have time. - No, you don't! Tomorrow is too late."

"You said a few times I wasn't a good provider. I didn't understand at first. I provided you with food, took care of your rent several times, gave you money to get the animals groomed, often paid for your gas, brought you a car, and was going to give you my SUV, but I wasn't providing love. I wasn't providing an emotional connection anymore. Our intimacy was fading, and it was all my fault. Since I got my hormones back to normal levels, I really understand how you feel now. I long for your touch, your hugs, your kisses now."

Isabella turns to look at the sun starting to set, looks back at Xander, and then emotionally asks, "Are you finished?"

"No, I have little more written down," Xander says as he starts reading again. "A few weeks before you left. You would argue with me. I'm living in poverty, and I would answer no; it's just a construction zone. What was I thinking about having my wife live in such conditions? I didn't know what to do. We had so many animals. I couldn't rent a house anywhere. Honestly, I was looking around before we moved out there in June. Remember, we looked into renting a house together with your parents, and that turned out to be a rental scam."

Xander stops, looks down at his papers, pulls out a different note, stops reading, and then says, "This is the note you left on our bed. You said you thought our Marriage was a mistake. The mistake was me not listening to you. The mistake was that we were on our phones at night too much. Mostly me. The mistake was that I didn't go to get my hormones checked out a year earlier. How we communicated with one another when we were upset was a mistake. A mistake was me not being the man I should have been for you. I understand that now. Our love and our connection, our passion about life when we first met, was not a mistake."

Xander turns and looks over at the temple and says. "Sun is setting behind the temple now,"

"Are you done?" Isabella asks as she turns her chair around to face the Temple.

"Yes," Xander says as he turns his chair to face the sunset.

"Can I have another glass of wine?" Isabella asks as Toon walks by.

Xander turns around and motions for Toon. "Can I have a beer Singha, please?" And then asks Isabella. "I thought you weren't going to drink?"

Isabella looks at the sun setting with a grin on her face, ignoring Xander's question.

7:05 as Xander looks at his phone. He turns to Isabella and asks, "Are you ready to go?"

Isabella just nods her head as she stands up to walk downstairs.

Outside the entrance of the Sala Rattanakosin Eatery and Bar

Isabella quickly walks out the door as Xander follows behind. "Hey, slow down, please," Xander says as he tries to catch up.

Isabella turns around and yells, "Why did you bring this shit up here?" as she turns back to walk away.

"Where are you going?" Xander asks as he catches up and grabs her left wrist.

Isabella twists her wrist, breaking Xander's grip, and yells, "Get your fucking hands off of me!" Then she turns around and punches Xander in the chest.

Xander stops and puts both of his hands up, palms facing Isabella, and takes a step back. "Hey, sorry," he says defensively. "This whole trip, you have been making small innuendos about me."

"Well, this whole trip, you have often been flirting with me!" She angrily comments, "Why can't you understand that we are just friends, nothing more?" She turns around and walks away from Xander.

"What are you planning on walking back to the hotel or something?" Xander asks as he starts to follow her.

Isabella turns around and starts walking backward, "Stop following me!" she yells as she takes a few more steps. "I can get my own taxi back."

Xander stops as she gets more distance from him. "Let's just get a taxi together, please," Xander says in a calm voice.

Isabella is still slowly walking backward away from Xander. When he notices a motorbike swerve towards her, "Isabella, watch out!" Xander points frantically as the passenger on the back of the motorbike reaches out with his right hand to grab Isabella's purse.

Isabella turns slightly to her left and then gets hit with a very hard jerk as her purse slides off her shoulder, knocking her to the ground.

Xander looks distraught as he sees Isabella lose her balance and start to fall. "Nooooooooo!" He yells at the top of his lungs as he notices Isabella catching herself from falling totally on the ground. He now turns his attention to the motorbike that is trying to speed away. Xander steps off the curb onto the street, as the motorbike is only a few feet away, coming towards him. As they swerve to avoid Xander, he reaches out with both hands, grabs the right side of the handlebar, and gives it a huge yank. The motorcyclist loses control of the motorbike as it does a hard right turn, smashing into a parked taxi and crashing the motorbike down on the street.

Xander is pulled to the ground from the weight of the motorbike. He quickly gets to his feet and approaches the thieves. The snatcher/passenger with Izzy's purse still in his hand gets to his feet first and turns around toward Xander. Before he can act, Xander throws the hardest push kick he has ever thrown into the snatcher's stomach, knocking him backward onto the motorbike that is lying on its side. The snatcher falls backward over the motorbike tire, flat on his back.

Xander turns to the motorcyclist/driver lying on the ground who is trying to free his foot that is pinned under the motorbike. Xander lets out a huge grunt as he stomps on the motorbike several times.

"Jab! Thai for pain or hurt!" The driver yells, and then he frees his leg.

Xander steps back and turns to the snatcher, who has gotten back to his feet and is still holding Isabella's purse. Snatcher removes his helmet and swings it at Xander, nearly missing his face. Xander can see out the corner of his eye as Isabella runs over to help. She approaches the snatcher from behind and grabs her purse out of his hand. He turns around and punches Isabella on the left side of the head as she steps backward away from the snatcher.

"Izzzzzzzy!" Xander yells as he sees her move away. Xander then takes a step forward, putting his hands around the snatcher's head in a Thai boxing clinch, pulling his head down. He kicked him multiple times with his right knee to his mid-section. He then lets go with his right hand while still holding with his left. Xander throws multiple right elbows into his face.

"Xander, watch out for the other guy," Isabella screams.

Xander looks over to his right while still clinching the snatcher. He turns the snatcher to his right in a pulling action so that the snatcher is between the driver and himself (That way, he won't get attacked from behind). He then steps with his right leg off to the left side of the snatcher. Xander then places his left leg behind the snatcher's left leg and trips him down, crashing him into the street. Knocking him unconscious. Before Xander can catch his balance from the leg trip, the driver punches Xander on the side of the face. Xander regains his balance, slightly bends at his waist, and head-butts the driver directly on the nose. "Crunch" as his nose is flattened and begins to bleed. The driver puts his hands on his nose and yells in pain. Xander puts both hands on his chest and gives him a hard shove. Just then, the driver trips over his bike onto the ground.

A small crowd of people gathered, and traffic stopped because of the motorbike in the street. Xander looks at the driver, who is still lying on the ground, holding his nose. Then he looks over to the snatcher, who is now sitting up, still dazed from having the back of his head hit the ground. Xander looks over to Isabella and asks, "Are you OK?" as he steps off the street back on the sidewalk.

"Yeah, I'm OK," she says as she brushes some of the dirt off Xander's back. "I've been hit harder at sparing." Isabella laughs, then asks, "What about you? Are you Ok?

"My hand is hurting from when I grabbed their bike and made them crash," he answers as they both start walking away from the crash.

"Ra-wang, ra-wang!" Thai for look out, as some of the Thais who have gathered yell at Xander and Isabella.

Isabella turns around and can see the snatcher has run up behind Xander, and is about to hit him with his helmet. "Xander, watch out!" She screams.

"Thump!" As Isabella watches, Xander gets hit in the back of the head with the helmet. He instantly goes limp as he collapses to the ground. Isabella tries her best to catch Xander as he falls to his knees and then forward onto his chest, hitting his forehead on the pavement. The snatcher grabs Isabella's hair and starts to pull it. Seconds later, the restaurant staff and security grab the snatcher and yank him away as Isabella throws a straight left to his face.

"Oh my God, Help!" Isabella frantically screams as she quickly kneels to check on Xander's lifeless body lying face down on the sidewalk. "Come on, babe, wake up," she says as she gently rolls him over to his back. "Wake up," as she puts his head into her lap.

A few of the Thais and one foreigner who have gathered around come to give assistance. "He took a very hard hit to the back of the head," the foreigner comments in a heavy German accent.

Isabella starts to cry as she desperately tries to wake him up. "Xander, please wake up, please!" as tears start to roll down her face. A tear drips off her cheek and falls onto Xander's forehead, and then another on his lips. She starts to see Xander move his eyes.

The German Foreigner grabs Xander's wrist and starts checking his pulse. "Pulse is good." He says.

"Can I have some water please?" Isabella asks as she looks at some of the people who are trying to help. She notices a Thai woman handing her a bottle of water. Isabella grabs the water and pours a little water over his forehead. "Come on, babe," she says as she is still crying.

"Ummmm," Xander moans as his eyes start to open up.

"Come on, get up," Isabella desperately pleads as she looks into his eyes, which are now glaring up at hers.

"What happened?" Xander asks as he starts to move his head.

"One of the guys you fought against attacked you from behind," Isabella answers as she helps Xander sit up.

Xander reaches out his hand and grabs the German man's hand as he helps him up to his feet. "How long have I been out?" Xander asks as he rubs the back of his head and then touches the bump on his forehead.

"You were unconscious for a few minutes," Isabella answers as she stands up and suggests, "Let's get a taxi and go to the hospital."

"I don't think I need to go to the hospital," Xander says as he looks at Isabella, "You got your purse back," he says as he gives out a small laugh. "Let's get out of here," Xander says as he grabs Isabella's hand to flag a taxi.

8:07 pm hotel room

"Hey, I'm going to take a long hot shower and just relax in the room tonight," Xander says as they enter the room.

"You really scared me," Isabella says as she puts her purse on her bed.

"I would have given my life to protect you," Xander explains as he looks in the mirror at the bump on his forehead.

"I know you would have," she answers, looks at Xander, and smiles. "While you're taking a shower, I'm going to change clothes and walk down, get a banana pancake, and maybe go to the cigar place again," she explains

"OK, please be careful," Xander says as he walks into the bathroom.

Isabella pokes her head into the bathroom as Xander takes his shirt off and says, "You were my hero tonight."

Isabella returns to the room a little after 10 pm and can hear the TV. She grabs the remote, turns the TV off, and mumbles to herself, "I hate it when he leaves the TV on in bed."

Xander turns over and asks, "How was your pancake?"

"Sorry if I woke you up," she comments as she looks at the icebag on the nightstand. "How's your head?" She asks.

"It's sore, but I don't think I have a concussion," Xander answers as he sits up in bed.

"That's good; I was concerned about you while I walked to Khaosan Road," Isabella explains as she walks over to check on Xander's forehead.

"I will be OK; I have had worse in fighting," Xander says as he touches Isabella's hand. "Have a good night," as Xander snuggles back into bed.

Isabella grabs her towel from the balcony and walks back into the room.

"Can you make sure you close the curtain tonight," Xander asks.

"Yes, you have a good night," Isabella says as she closes the curtain.

Chapter 8: Phone Call Home

6:00 am Isabella's alarms vibrate on her phone, waking her up. She sits up and looks over at Xander, who has his back toward her, lying in the fetal position, still sleeping. She quietly puts on her shorts and T-shirt and goes into the bathroom. After a few minutes, she comes out of the bathroom and sees Xander still asleep. Isabella grabs Xander's phone from the nightstand and puts a handwritten note in its place. As she turns, she sees Xander's clothes, which he had on from last night, lying on the ground. She notices the papers he read from lying on the ground, along with a few Thai coins and his wallet. Isabella reaches down, grabs the folded papers, and puts them into her back pocket. Looks over at Xander, who is still asleep. She grabs her bible and her Lonely Planet book and exits out of the room.

6:23 am Hotel lobby

"Morning," Isabella says as she walks up to the front desk and starts to show the receptionist a map of the Khaosan Road area from her Lonely Planet tour book. "Where is this park?" She asks, referring to a park next to the river.

Ploy, the receptionist, answers. "This park is very near, a 5-minute walk, ka." Ploy walks out from behind the booth and motions for Isabella to follow her. Ploy points down the alley towards the river and says, "Turn right at the main road and it's a two or three minute walk. Ka." As Ploy turns around to walk back to the front desk.

"Khop Khun Ka," Isabella says in Thai, meaning thank you.

Ploy wai (bow) Isabella and says, "Mimi payha ka," no problem in Thai.

Isabella grabs one of the business cards off the desk and says to Ploy, "I'm in room 302. If my friend comes down, please tell him I will be back at noon." She then turns and starts walking toward the alley.

Isabella comes to the end of the alley, turns right, and can see the park from a distance. She continues walking and comes to several street food vendors set up along the road. She notices one selling Thai coffee.

Isabella places an order and watches the Thai man get a ladle of coffee from a big metal pot with a small fire under it. He pours the coffee from the ladle into a coffee cup. Then he gets another coffee cup and holds it down about one foot under the first cup as he pours the coffee into the second cup. Then he repeats. Pours second cup into the first cup. And finally, pours the coffee into a paper coffee cup. Then, he points to a can of condensed milk and sugar. Isabella shakes her head no and gives him 20 baht.

She continues walking towards the park. She crosses the street and then enters the park. The park is nothing special; just an open lawn measuring 100ft by 400ft with a few trees, but on the banks of the river. Isabella takes a seat on a park bench and takes a sip of her coffee. A bitter expression appears on her face as she whispers to herself, "This is some strong coffee!" and takes another small sip. She reaches into her pockets and pulls out Xander's papers, which were lying on the floor. She unfolds the papers and notices that on one side it has something printed out. On the backside are handwritten notes and a few paragraphs expressing the breakup. As she turns the page, she sees the breakup letter she wrote to him. Isabella then folds the three sheets of paper up and slides it under her bottom on the bench.

Isabella looks up to her right and notices a few older Thai people doing Tai chi. She takes a deep breath, looks down, and opens the bible to read. After a few minutes, she closes the bible and pulls out the papers again. She unfolds the first page and begins to read the top paragraph, which is from an internet site.

(God Driven Men)

"Take ownership of your thoughts, feelings, and emotions. Strong men don't need to blame their wives for how they feel and react. Your marriage is the same as a business; it takes strong leadership, strategy, and consistent effort, but most men approach their marriage reactively, not proactively. We focus on more work and working harder while ignoring our wife's emotional needs. Would you ignore your teammates or business partners' concerns about the business? Then why would you shut down when your wife expresses her emotional needs? Would you operate your business with no clear goal or objective? Then why are you coasting in your marriage without any direction or goals? Most marriages don't end because of one huge event but from neglect and mismanagement, which is the same as why a lot of businesses fail and the ability to adapt. 50% of marriages fail, and in second marriages, the percentage is even higher. So, take control of who you are. You can't lead your wife until you can lead yourself. Let's begin our journey on making you the man God intended you to be for your wife."

Isabella puts the paper down and gets Xander's phone out of her pocket. 7:07 am, as she checked the time and then dialed her mom.

"Hello," Isabella's mom answers.

"Hey, it's Izzy, your daughter calling you from Thailand again," Isabella says as she gets up to walk closer to the river so she can hear better on the phone.

"How are you and Xander doing? Are you guys still having a great time?" Mom asks.

"Mom, I don't know how to tell you this, but Xander got hurt last night," Isabella says as she sits down on the grass next to the riverbank.

"Oh my God! What happened?" She exclaims on the phone.

"Last night, we had a small argument, and as I was walking away from Xander. My purse got snatched by two guys on a motorbike," Isabella explained.

"What!" Mother frantically asks. "Are you Ok?

"Yes, I'm fine, but I did skin up my arm a little when I fell down," Isabella says, then pauses, "Xander jumped into the road and caused the motorbike to crash."

"Is that where he got hurt?" Mother asks.

"No, Xander took on both guys on the motorbike! It was like something you see in a movie," Isabella expresses. "I got punched by the guy who grabbed my purse, but I'm fine."

"What! So how did Xander get hurt?" She asks.

"Xander knocked out one guy and hurt the other one very badly," Isabella explains. "Xander thought the fight was over, and we started walking away, and the guy who he knocked out woke up and attacked Xander from behind." Pause.

"Mom -it was horrible!" Isabella says as she starts to cry a little. "Mom, for a split second, I thought he was dead, and then I could see him breathing, but he didn't move for about two minutes." She sniffles. "It was really scary!"

"Well, what happened? How did he get hurt?" Mom asks.

"The guy grabbed his motorbike helmet and hit him with it in the back of the head," Isabella says and then mentions, "He collapsed in my arms similar to how I collapsed last year at Bonnaroo."

"Did you go to the hospital?" Mother eagerly asks.

"No, he said he would be OK after he got up. So, we took a taxi back to the hotel and got him an icepack," Isabella states. "We talked a little before we went to bed. He was still sleeping this morning when I got up."

Isabella can hear her mom yelling in the distance at the dogs and can hear her grabbing the phone again. "Sorry about that. The dogs were barking. You know how they are sometimes," Isabella's mom explains. "Well, I'm glad he is not hurt very bad." Then the mother asks, "What were you two arguing about?"

"We were at a very nice place having dinner, and he pulls out this paper and starts reading off of it. Honestly, I didn't pay attention to half of it, but he had the letter I gave to him when I moved out. For some reason, it made me upset," Isabella explains.

"Did he say something bad or insulting to you?" She asks.

"No, pretty much that he understood why I left," Isabella answers, then pauses, takes a deep breath and asks her mom. "Do you think I made a mistake?"

"What do you mean?" Mother asks.

"I mean leaving Xander. Like, should I have moved out temporarily or given him an ultimatum or something?" Isabella asks.

"You know that's not my decision to make. It's been hard on everyone. We loved him, and I'm sure his family loves you," Isabella's moms explained. "What made you want to talk about this now?" She asks.

"I often think about him from time to time. But last night, when he jumped in the street and fought those guys. I started looking at him like the man I fell in love with. And when he got knocked out. I thought that I lost him." Isabella reflects.

"I see," Mother says.

"Also, I grabbed all of his notes off the floor this morning and started reading some of it?" Isabella says.

"Grab his papers?!" Mother asks.

"Yeah, I grabbed them mainly because I wanted to burn the letter I wrote to him. Then, I was sitting there reading the bible for a while. I was curious, so I started looking at some of the things that were written down and some of the information that was printed out on it," Isabella clarifies.

"What was some of the information printed out?" Mom asks.

"The first thing I read was a program about making men better leaders with their wives called (God Driven Men) and the other things I just glanced at, mostly about improving yourself and steps to become a better person. Another thing I looked at was something about different personality disorders. Antisocial, Avoidant, Borderline, Dependent, Histrionic, Narcissistic, Obsessive, Paranoid." Isabella states.

"Yes, he told me about some of those things he has been reading and a couple of the counselors he has talked to. We talked about different personalities. Me and Xander have a similar personality, and you and your dad share similar personalities," mother explains.

"Really, he talked about some of these things with you. Did he say what type of personality he thinks I am?" Isabella asks.

Mother begins to answer, "Xander told me from his research that everyone can share all these personalities, but usually, one is more dominant. He said you have a few of the Avoidant traits, which is one of the hardest to show forgiveness, and some of the Obsessive, and he had some sort of Anxious and Dependent personality."

"Why is he learning about this?" Isabella asks.

"If he had learned some of these things before, he could have approached conversations better with you," Mother comments then continues. "Every human has different personality disorders. Learning how to communicate with a different personality other than your own is important. We often talk to our spouse like their personality is the same as our own. That's what Xander shared with me."

Silence

"Are you still there?" Mother asks.

"Yeah, sorry. I was reading some of the things he had written down. Not sure if he was just writing stuff down or something he wanted to express to me, and one seemed to be out of anger," Isabella comments.

"Well, I'm sure if he wanted to share it with you. He would have done it by now," Isabella's mom states.

"Yeah, I guess you're right. I shouldn't read anymore. But I am still going to burn the letter I wrote," Izzy expresses.

Isabella's mom laughs on the phone and says, "One of the mistakes that I think you guys made was getting all those darn animals! That had to be very stressful for both of you guys. Xander had to build barns and fences and try to work on the cabin and his work, too. He had more patience than me! And you often had to take care of the animals, too, and you had to shut your business down. I know that put you under a lot of stress as well."

"Yeah. And starting the generator got old too," Isabella says.

"I really think you liked it at first and had high hopes. You were able to walk Dali down to the creek and take the goats on walks. Your chickens could run around. You were able to plant flowers and have a garden," Mother comments.

"You guys just made mistakes in communication. I can see you were truly in love with him," Mom says, then asks, "Remember a few years ago when I and your dad had some problems?"

Mother continues, "We almost split up, but we were able to work it out. Neither one of us gave up," Isabella's mother states.

"Yeah, I remember," Isabella answers.

"Xander told me a story from one of the counselors he talks to a few times. About a married couple that had a few problems." Mother begins the story, "His wife wanted to file for a divorce. She was very unhappy with her husband and asked a Christian lawyer if she could make the breakup and divorce as painful as possible. The lawyer said if you make the breakup difficult, he will welcome a divorce. So, the lawyer devised a plan. He instructed the wife to return home and not mention that they talked or bring up anything about a divorce. Be as nice as you can and put everything back into marriage. After three months, come back and see me, and we will serve him the divorce papers. That will totally devastate him. Three months later, the attorney calls the lady and asks if you are ready to file the divorce papers. She tells the lawyer, no, it won't be necessary any longer. We were able to work everything out."

Isabella pauses, then starts to say, "Xander doesn't even have a home for me to stay and I'm not moving back into the cabin."

"About one month ago, Xander said even if you guys did reconcile, he wouldn't want you to move back into the cabin anyways," Isabella's mom explains.

"He really said that," Izzy comments.

"He said he is building a real house out there now. I'm not sure how far along it is. Last we talked, he was working on the septic system. And he said he wants to work on himself more," Mom explains.

Izzy sighs and says, "Mom, I don't know what to do!"

"What would it hurt if you started slow or just went on a few small dates? You have already moved out. He lived with us for almost three years. So him coming over to visit you wouldn't be a problem. But this is something you need to decide, not us. We will support your decision no matter what you decide. I just want you to be happy," Mom explains, then pauses. "I'm glad you were able to go on this trip because until now, you haven't done anything except go to your room when you're not working. I know you don't have many friends, and I know Xander was your best friend. But you need to go out and try to socialize when you get home," the mother expresses.

"Mom, I'm afraid that if I try to open my heart, he will just go back to the same old routine," Isabella comments.

"Some people can change if they have experienced a lot of anguish or pain. If he can do the same routine long enough, it will become a habit," Mom says

"I know. I know," Isabella answers.

"Well, Mom, I probably need to let you go. Going to run out of minutes on the phone soon," Isabella says as she stands up off the lawn in the park.

"How much does it cost to call me?" Mom asks.

"I think Xander said like $1.25, $1.50 a minute," answers Isabella.

"Wow, that's expensive. Well, I love you. Tell Xander we will be praying for him and see you in a few days," Mom says.

"I love you, Mom," Isabella says as she hangs up the phone and then pulls out her lighter.

8:37 am back at the hotel.

Xander wakes up and is feeling confused because of getting KO the night before. He looks over and doesn't see Isabella. Scratches his head and gets up to go pee. After he returns, he goes to grab his phone off the nightstand to see what time it is. He looks around, moving the note Isabella placed there. Then he looks under the bed. "What the hell?" he mumbles to himself. He then feels around on the bed and can't find his phone. He sits back down and looks at the nightstand again and notices the note that has (Xander) written on the front. He opens it up and begins to read.

"Xander, I hope you won't be upset, but I grabbed your phone to call my mom. Afterward, I'm going to have the morning to myself. Please go ahead and get breakfast or lunch, depending on how late you slept in. I will meet you in the lobby at noon. Isabella."

Xander yawns as he scratches his head and says to himself, "Well, shit." Xander gets up and goes into the bathroom to take a shower and start his day.

9:07 am hotel lobby

Xander walks up to the front desk and asks Ploy, "Have you seen my lady friend?"

"She walked to the park next to the river 3 hours ago. Ka," Ploy politely answers and says, "She said she would be back here at noon. Ka"

"Ok, thank you." Xander comments back to Ploy and then talks to himself. "I guess I will get breakfast here at the café."

12:10 pm Café at the hotel

Isabella returns to the hotel, peeks in the lobby, and doesn't see Xander. She starts to walk towards the stairs when she hears Ploy yell for her. "Excuse me if you're looking for your friend. He is in the café. Ka"

Isabella wai at Ploy and turned around to head toward the café. As she enters, she can see Xander sitting in the corner of the café reading the Bangkok Post. She quietly walks up to him, puts her hand on top of the newspaper, and pulls it down a little. "Hey," Isabella says, and she hands him his phone.

"How is your mom?" Xander asks as he puts the newspaper down.

"She is doing good," Isabella says as she pulls her chair out to sit down.

"What time did you get up this morning?" Xander asks as he puts his hand on his coffee cup.

"It was around 6:00 am, and then I walked down to a small park by the river," Isabella answers.

"I think I know what park you're talking about; it's around 10 mins away, and it's very small with a few park benches," Xanders comments.

"Yes, that's the one. I got a street coffee, called my mom, read the bible for a while, and soaked up some sun." She smiles and then asks, "How are you feeling?

"Head and neck are a little sore. My hand feels the worst, but I think I'm good. Probably not going out dancing tonight," Xander says, then chuckles.

Isabella smiles, stands back up, and expresses, "Hey, I want to get a facial and a massage, then get some alone time if that's OK."

"Yes, that's fine; you're free to do what you want," Xander states, taking a sip of his coffee and grabbing his phone.

"I'm going to go back to the room, then head out. Do you want to meet me back here at 5 pm and make plans for dinner?" Isabella asks.

"Sounds good to me," Xander says as he looks up at Isabella and gives her a small smile.

Isabella takes a few steps away and says. "Hey, thank you for last night. You didn't hesitate and showed no fear."

Xander just looks and smiles as he looks back at his phone.

Isabella returns to the room and notices Xander's clothes from the night before are still lying in the same place. She gets Xander's notes from her pocket and is about to drop them on the floor and stops. "What else did he write about?" She thinks to herself and sits down on the corner of the bed. Opens the paper, and she notices some scribble and eraser marks on the back. And several written paragraphs, one being what Xander read to her last night. Then, she begins reading the first one.

"Isabella, you were my one true love. I've been waiting 25 years to find you. And somewhere on our journey together, a lot of mistakes were made. Your limerence for me has faded; I understand that now. Sorry, I didn't take the necessary steps to be the man you needed me to be until after you left. Sorry I didn't give you the breakup at first. Somewhere along our journey together, you became part of my identity, and part of me died when you left. I see now that you being my best friend wasn't enough. I have…"

Isabela can't make out the last part of the paragraph because it's been scratched out. And begins to read a few notes written about extroverts and introverts. Then, she starts reading the next paragraph.

"Sorry I didn't give you the breakup and talked to your family and a few friends. I understand that now it was the wrong thing to do. It has a lot to do with our personalities. You're an introvert, and you want to sit with your internal thoughts and feelings. While I'm an extrovert who openly expresses my feelings and thoughts. Also, I consider your parents my close friends and love them as my own." Before she can finish the rest of the paragraph, she hears the door handle jiggle. She quickly folds the paper up and drops it on the floor near Xander's clothes as Xander walks in the door.

"You scared me! I thought you already left," Xander says in a surprised tone.

Isabella looks down, kicks the folded papers under the bed, looks up, and says. "Hey! I was just dropping off my books. See you at 5 pm." As she gets up and quickly walks out the door.

"OK, have a nice relaxing time," Xander comments, then moves out of the way to let Isabella pass.

4:58 pm Hotel Lobby

Xander steps out of the alley into the hotel lobby and sees Isabella sitting down. He walks over and notices she has already changed clothes for the evening, and he then asks, "How was your facial and massage?"

"Well, can you tell?" Isabella says as she looks at him and smiles.

"Tell what?" Xander comments.

"My facial, what you think," She comments.

"Ahhh." As Xander is staring at Isabella's face, then says, "Yeah, I can tell under your eyes."

"Anything else?" She says as she starts blinking her eyes and smiles.

"Oh, you got eyelash extensions. Looks great on you," Xander says, then steps back. "I need to run up to the room and put on some different clothes."

"OK, I'm ready for dinner," Isabella expresses.

Xander returns 10 min later, and Isabella asks him, "What's our plan for dinner?"

"I called Dominique, and he is going to come here and meet us for dinner," Xander explains.

"You never said where we are going," Isabella comments as she stands up.

"Sorry, Dominique suggested a French Thai Restaurant. I think it's around the corner from here called (Madame Musur). I told him what happened last night, and I said I didn't want to go far," Xander explains.

Isabella looks in the mirror and then says, "I think we walked past it the first night we were here walking to Khaosan Road." She then looks at Xander and asks, "Are you ready?"

Xander nods, then asks, "So how was your massage?" as they make a right out of the hotel.

"It was so relaxing. They were able to work out a kink in my shoulders," she explains. "What did you do the last couple hours?" Isabella asks.

"Actually, I got a foot massage and pedicure. My head hurts a little, and I didn't want to do anything strenuous," Xander answers and then says, "We have to make a left here."

Isabella makes a left with Xander, and then she points straight ahead and comments. "Hey, I see the sign for the restaurant."

"Where?" Xander asks.

"Right in front of us behind the Beer Chang sign," Isabella clarifies.

"This restaurant is very close," Xanders says to Isabella

Xander walks up to the hostess and asks, "Table for 4, please."

"I don't see Dominique," Isabella comments in Xander's ear as they follow the hostess.

"I think we are a little early," Xander says as he grabs his phone to look at the time. "It is 5:48."

Xander and Isabella ordered an appetizer and two glasses of wine. And then Xander looks over at Isabella and says, as he lifts his wine glass, "Here's to our last night in Bangkok."

Isabella lifts her glass, gently touches Xander's glass, and smiles.

Moments later.

"Dominique is here," Xander says as he stands up to greet him.

"Oh, sorry I'm late. Traffic jam," Dominique says as he looks at Xander's bruise on his forehead, then leans in and kisses Xander on each cheek.

Dominique turns to Isabella and says, "Sava bien," and comes up behind her, kisses her on the cheek and turns back to Xander.

"Oh, my friend. So good you come back to Thailand. Too bad you couldn't stay longer," Dominique says to Xander as he grabs the menu and takes a seat.

"I wish we could stay longer, too, but we both have jobs and things we need to take care of back home," Xander expresses.

"So, Dominique, your wife couldn't make it tonight?" Isabella asks.

"Non non (French for no) she was not feeling good," Dominique answers.

The waitress comes to the table, and they order food. Then, Dominique orders a round of shots.

Isabella looks at Xander and whispers in his ear, "I didn't really want to drink tonight."

Xander whispers back, "It's our last night here, and we didn't kill each other so we can celebrate," Xander leans back and then laughs.

Isabella smiles back at Xander.

The waitress brings out three shots and gives them to Dominique.

Dominique hands Xander and Isabella a shot, lifts his shot in the air, and then says in French, "Acclamations."

"Cheers," Xander and Isabella say back.

"This is very good; what is this?" Isabella asks Dom.

"It's a famous liquor from Corsica called Chartreuse," Dominique answers and looks at the waitress for three more.

"What is it made from?" She asks.

"It's made from herbs and berries," Dominique answers.

After dinner, Isabella looks at Xander's phone and says to Xander, "It's 7:20 pm. I think I'm going to leave you two alone and go walk around for some more gifts for my parents." Then she stands up.

"What? You're leaving?" Xander surprisingly says, then stands up.

"Yeah, I don't want to drink anymore and want sometime to myself to think," Isabella says as she walks over to Dominique to give him a hug.

"I'm not going to be out very long myself," Xander says to Isabella as he gets up to walk Isabella to the entrance.

"You don't need to escort me to the door. Go to your friend," Isabella comments.

Xander stops and then says, "We've got to get up early tomorrow and pack," and turns around to sit with Dominque.

"Isabella seems like a wonderful woman; I'm so happy for you," Dominique expresses as he looks at the waitress for two more shots.

"Yes, she is a wonderful woman, but I hate to tell you this. She walked out of marriage in October and moved back in with her parents," Xander comments, then looks at Dom with a grin.

"Bro, I'm sorry to hear that," Dominique says as he gives him a pat on his shoulder.

"I was hoping this trip would spark something again, but a couple of nights ago, I could tell she was still not interested in a relationship," Xander says as he grabs the shot.

"Here is to love that we have lost," Dominique says as he lifts his shot glass.

Xander takes a deep breath and tells Dominique, "It really affected my mental health for about three months, but I vowed never to let this happen again. The first month, I prayed all the time. But then I was listening to a Christian-based marriage counselor on YouTube. He said you must do more than just study scripture. Faith without work is dead. So I study and study and study about men and women and how to listen to be a better husband and, hopefully, one day, a better father."

"Wee, I see," Dominique comments and puts his arms around Xander, kisses him on the cheek, and says, "I love you, Bro. You're a good man. Most men who lose their love start going crazy for a while. Drinking or drugs or stop working out, start stalking their ex. Good, you start making positive changes."

"Thank you, Dom. She must see that I am a man of high value again. Someone of great worth, but I need to do this for myself as well," Xander says, then gets a drink of water and comments. "This trip to Bangkok might be our last trip together," Xander sighs. "I don't want to talk about her anymore. I just want her to be happy."

"I love you, bro," Dominique says as he puts his arm around Xander's shoulder again.

Dominique and Xander had a few more beers, then continued to talk about old times for another hour and say their goodbyes.

"Thank you, my friend, for coming to the gym and inviting me for dinner; maybe next time you can stay longer," Dominique expresses.

"Thanks for coming out here tonight and joining me and Isabella for dinner. Love you, Dominique," Xander says as they both embrace one last time.

As they walk into the alley, Dominique opens a taxi door and turns to Xander, who is walking away and yells. "You will always be a warrior; always keep your head up."

Xander turns around, puts both fists in the air like a boxing stance, smiles, and turns to start walking back to the hotel.

Xander gets back to the empty room a little after 9 pm and takes a shower. Then climbs into bed, starts watching the news on his phone, and then falls asleep.

The door handle jiggles, and the door opens as Isabella quietly walks into the room. Xander wakes up and asks, "Hey, everything OK? What time is it?" Xander says while lying on his left side.

"I'm fine. It's like 10:20. Sorry to wake you up," Isabella answers as she goes into the bathroom to shower.

After an extremely long shower, Isabella comes out of the bathroom with a towel wrapped around her in a dark bedroom. Isabella uses the flashlight on her phone to maneuver herself around without tripping. Takes the towel off, throws it on the floor, pulls back the comforter, slides behind Xander in the same bed, and wraps her right arm around his body. Xander is awakened by her moist body pressing up against his back and says. "What are you doing?"

Isabella gently holds Xander with her arm and comments, "Shhhhh, don't turn over. Please go back to sleep." She holds him and goes to sleep.

Chapter 9: Going Home

8:00 am alarm rings on Xander's phone as he opens his eyes and raises up. He rolls over and sees Isabella is no longer in the room. Xander then sits up and looks over at Isabella's bed and notices she has already begun packing some of her things. Still half asleep, he stumbles out of bed, walks into the bathroom, and steps into the shower. While taking a shower, Xander can hear the front door of their room shut. "Izzy, is that you?" Xander shouts.

"Of course it is; who else?" She yells back.

"Be out in a couple of minutes," Xander shouts back.

Isabella walks over to the balcony and opens the curtain to let the sunlight into the room. Soon after, she can hear the shower being turned off. Xander steps out of the bathroom with a towel wrapped around his waist. "I got you a coffee," Isabella says as she starts folding more of her clothes.

"Thank you," Xander says as he grabs his cup and then asks, "What time did you get up this morning?"

"I got up at 7 am and went down to the café and read the bible for a while," Isabella answers.

"That's good," Xanders says as he looks for something to wear and comments, "Remember, we need to be at the airport at 3 pm today."

Isabella frowns, then comments, "Yeah, I know; I wish we could have stayed longer and gone down to the islands."

Xander grabs some clothes and starts walking to the bathroom when Isabella says, "Hey, about last night," and before she can finish her sentence, Xander cuts her off.

"Don't worry, I understand. You had too many shots," he says as he shuts the door.

"No, that's not what I was going to say," she comments back.

"Sorry, I couldn't understand what you said," Xander shouts.

"Never mind," Isabella shouts back and mumbles under her breath.

Xander steps out of the bathroom fully dressed and asks, "What do you want to do today?"

"I'm open to anything," she comments, then says, "Probably not a good idea to do something where we get all sweaty." Then she asks, "How's your head?"

"It's still sore to touch. When I bend over, I can feel some pressure, but I don't think I have a concussion," he says as he grabs his luggage bag and places it on the bed.

"Two minutes is a long time to be knocked out," Isabella answers as she watches Xander grab his dirty clothes off the floor and place them into a dirty laundry bag. She thinks to herself, "I hope he doesn't notice his notes under the bed."

Xander turns to her and says, "I'm going to leave one set of clothes out to change in right before we leave."

Isabella smiles and comments to herself, "Good, he didn't even notice," and looks up, then says, "I'm going to do the same."

"You want to go down to the café and get breakfast," Xander asks.

"I think they have pancakes on the menu," Isabella says as if she starts walking toward the door.

"I loved that pancake place we went to in Gatlinburg next to the alleyway," Xander comments as he follows behind Isabella.

"Are you talking about the one where we had to wait in line for 1hr in the cold?" She comments as she starts walking down the stairs.

"That's the one, and it was near that little Irish bar we went to, where they could make pictures in the froth of your beer," Xander explains.

They step off the stairs into the lobby, and Xander tells Isabella, "Hey, get us a table. I am going to ask the front desk if we can check out a little later before we go to the airport."

Isabella nods her head and walks into the café.

"You want to walk down to the park next to the river?" Xander asks as they finish breakfast.

"Sounds good to me," Isabella answers, then states, "I want to run back up to my room and grab my bible so I can read for a little while I'm there."

9:41 am Santi Chai Prakan Park

Isabella sits down next to a tree in the shade and puts her bible on her lap. "Are you sitting down?" she asks.

"I'm going to run across the street and get us some water," Xander says, then jogs away.

Five mins later, Xander returns and sees Isabella already reading. "Here is your water," Xander says as he sits down next to her.

"You can go do your YouTube thing or whatever you watch these days," Isabella remarks as she grabs the water. "Thank you."

"No, I'm good. It's our last day here. I want to spend time with my friend, not on my phone," Xander explains as he scoots closer to Isabella, then asks, "What book of the bible are you reading?"

"I've been reading about forgiveness in the Book of Colossians," Isabella answers as she looks at Xander and smiles.

"Would you care to read it to me, if you don't mind?" Xander asks.

Isabella starts to read Colossians 3:13, "Bear with one another and forgive any complaint you have against someone else. Forgive as the Lord forgave you." Then stops, looks at some notes she was using as a book marker and starts reading Ephesians 4:32, "Be kind to one another, tenderhearted, forgiving one another, as Christ forgave you." She takes a sip of water and asks, "You want me to keep going?

"Up to you," Xander answers and then states, "We should have done more things like this or put our heads together and co-author books together."

Isabella looks back, smiles, and starts reading from the book of Psalms. After reading for a few minutes, she looks up and sees Xander staring at her with a very attentive look. "What?" she asks.

"Nothing, I'm just listening to you," he answers.

Isabella smiles back and begins to read again.

Moments later, Xander leans back against the tree and says, "Sorry, my back was hurting."

"Mine is too, why don't you spread your legs open, and I can lean my back on your chest," Isabella comments as she turns around to lean up against Xander. She then begins reading again.

Around 10 min pass, and Isabella puts the bible down and asks, "What are you thinking about? You have been a little quiet this morning."

"Just thinking about the last few days," Xander says and sighs.

"I know it's our last day," she expresses; she then puts her right hand on the top of Xander's hand.

Xander looks down and softly moves his right hand back as Isabella's finger intertwines with his.

"Xander, I'm sorry how things turned out between us," Isabella confides.

Xander takes a few breaths and starts to outline some of his thoughts. "It took me a couple of months to find myself after being out there alone. I had to search deep into myself again and learn to be the man that God intended me to be. I realize I wasn't putting God first and my wife second. I'm the one who failed you. Luckily, you had your parents that you could depend on."

Isabella squeezes his hand a little tighter as they both just sit there quietly, looking out over the river for a couple of minutes.

"Sorry for trying to get your parents involved. I didn't have a lot of friends for support, and my family lives so far away. And on top of that. Your mom was diagnosed with cancer. It was tough for both of us," Xander explains.

Isabella lets go of Xander's hands, stands up, and then says, "It was very hard for me, too. I loved our animals and our little farm. The few friends that I have are your friends, too, and I really didn't know what to say to them. When I wasn't working, I stayed in my room a lot." Isabella then turns around and crouches over to grab the bible and continues, "Sometimes I would check on you on Facebook or Instagram. And wanted to reach out. Then you would say something to my mom about us, and it would make me upset again."

Xander stands up and comments, "Yeah, it took me a while to realize that. I know it took a lot of courage for you to move out. I prayed it could have happened differently, but you wouldn't have been able to help your mom as much if you stayed."

"Yeah, you know how close I am with my parents," Isabella utters as she stands back up.

"You know I have changed, and I'm in the process of actually building a real house on the property now," Xander expresses.

"Yes, I can see some of your changes," Isabella answers, then states, "My mom mentioned you're in the process of building another house." She then asks, "What are you going to do with the cabin?"

"I guess turn it into an office or storage or maybe even a guest bedroom or a doggy room, haha," Xander says as he starts walking to the river, then states, "No woman is going to take me seriously if I don't have a real house."

Isabella just looks at Xander with an unemotional face, then asks, "Where are you going?"

"Was going to sit down next to the river," Xander answers.

"You want to go back to Khaosan Road and walk around a little?" Isabella asks.

"Sure," Xander answers as he walks back to Isabella.

Isabella hooks her arm around Xander's arm, leans her head on his shoulders, and says, "I really miss talking to you." They start walking back to Khaosan Road.

12:02 pm Khaosan Road.

Xander and Isabella pass the banana pancake vendor, and Xander says, "Last chance for a banana pancake."

Isabella laughs "I'm pancaked out."

Xander laughs with her, then comments, "We got about 1hr to look around, and then we need to head back to the hotel."

Just then, Isabella spots a monkey doing tricks and then comes around collecting tips for its handler. Isabella walks over and squats down, gives the monkey a 10-baht coin, and turns to Xander and says, "Can we take him home?" She then stands up with her bible under her arm, puts her two index fingers together, and gives Xander a sad puppy dog look.

"Wish we could; I can see it now going through the X-ray machine at the airport," Xander comments as he hands Isabella the rest of his coins.

"I never got to see an elephant while I was here," Isabella expresses as they both continue walking along.

Xander leans over and comments in Isabella's ear, "When I first came here, you would quite often see an elephant walking around here with its trainer. You buy a banana from its handler, and then you would feed it to the elephant."

"Ahh, why didn't we go do that?" Isabella asks.

"While back, they outlawed it in Bangkok because of traffic and it being dangerous to the elephant; I think one got hit by a car," Xander explains, then points to a vendor selling coconut ice cream.

"Oh, poor elephant," she expresses.

After getting a cup of coconut ice cream and buying a few more gifts for their family and friends, they go back to the hotel to finish packing and check out.

1:24 pm Hotel Room.

"You mind if I take a shower first?" Isabella asks as they enter the room.

"Yeah, go ahead," Xander answers as he walks to the bed and starts placing his belongings into their bag. After a few minutes, he has everything packed except his toothbrush and clothes on his back.

Isabella takes a quick shower and steps out of the bathroom around 5 min later with a towel wrapped around herself and asks, "How are we doing on time?"

"Good," Xander answers as he grabs his clothes to fly home and walks to the bathroom.

Xander exits a few minutes later from the bathroom and sees Isabella struggling to get her clothes into the bag.

"Give me a hand, please," she gently asks.

Xander walks over, grabs the bag that got lost, places it on the floor, and instructs Isabella, "Stand on top of the bag while I zip it up."

"OK, there we go." Xander comments. Then asks, "Got your passport and tickets ready?"

"Check," She answers.

"Well, let's go down and get a Taxi," Xander comments.

3:07 pm Suvarnabhumi Airport

Isabella and Xander grab their bags and look for the Etihad counter. "This is a long line," Xander says as they queue in line.

"This will take forever," Isabella states.

"Yeah, I know," Xander answers back and says, "And we will still have to get our passport stamped."

Forty-five minutes later, Xander and Isabella finally check their bag and get their boarding pass. As they walk to customs, they notice another huge line. "Ahh shit," Xander comments.

"I'm getting worried," Isabella nervously says as she looks at the time on the wall.

4:12 pm.

"This line is moving much faster, but we are going to be cutting it close," Xander expresses, then says, "We are going to have to run to the terminal."

"I trust you," Isabella answers.

Twenty minutes later, Xander grabs his passport from immigration officers and sees Isabella waiting off to the side. "We are going to have to hustle," Xander comments.

"Let's do this!" Isabella eagerly answers as she throws the bag over her shoulder.

Xander and Isabella take off in a jog toward the terminal as they weave in and out of people.

Isabella notices the time on the Flight Information Displays and yells, "It's 4:50."

Xander yells back, "I think our terminal is past these restaurants."

A few moments later, they arrived at the terminal. Xander grabs his phone and looks at the time. 4:54. As they notice the flight is already boarding. "We barely made it." Xander expresses as he looks over at Isabella, breathing heavily, and asks, "You, OK?"

"You know I can't run fast with my lungs sometimes," she answers back as she is trying to catch her breath.

"Yeah, I know, but we made it," Xander comments as he pats Isabella on the back. "We are next."

Flight attendants check their tickets and ask, "One of you is having a vegetarian dinner, correct?"

Isabella raises her hand.

"Well, this is it," Xander says as they walk to the terminal ramp.

Isabella just looks and smiles as she follows Xander.

"You want the window seat?" Xander asks as they enter the plane.

"Window, but later on, we can change," Izzy states as she looks for the seat number.

Isabella hands her bag to Xander so he can put it in the overhead compartment. She slides in next to the window and sits down. Xander takes his phone out of his pocket, turns it off, and puts it in the bag. Then he places his bag in the overhead compartment and sits next to Isabella.

"This is your captain speaking. Thank you for flying Etihad Airlines. Our flight time to Abu Dhabi is approximately 7hr and 5 mins. Please watch the short safety video on the headrest in front of you. Thank you for flying with us. Flight Attendants, please make sure the cabin is secure."

The airplane moves away from the terminal and starts taxiing toward the runway. It makes its final turn and pauses for a second.

Isabella looks at Xander and says, "Hey! Look at me."

Xander turns his head, looks at Isabella, and smiles.

"Thank you for convincing me to go on this trip to Thailand with you; I had a really wonderful time," Isabella expresses just as the plane thrust forward, startling her. To her surprise, she reached down and grabbed Xander's hand on the armrest.

The jetliner lifts off, and Isabella is looking out the window as Thailand gets smaller and smaller.

The fasten seat belt sign turns off.

Isabella reclines her seat back and then leans over and gently kisses Xander on the cheek then softly says to him, "Let's talk more about us when we get home."

"I'm open to that," Xander says. "We can take it one day at a time." Xander then grabs Isabella's hand.

"I would like that," Isabella expresses, then lays her head on Xander's shoulder.

The end.

www.ingramcontent.com/pod-product-compliance
Lightning Source LLC
Chambersburg PA
CBHW071007280626
47160CB00015B/2029